SILENCED BY A SPELL

(A Lacey Doyle Cozy Mystery—Book Seven)

FIONA GRACE

Fiona Grace

Fiona Grace is author of the LACEY DOYLE COZY MYSTERY series, comprising nine books (and counting); of the TUSCAN VINEYARD COZY MYSTERY series, comprising six books (and counting); of the DUBIOUS WITCH COZY MYSTERY series, comprising three books (and counting); of the BEACHFRONT BAKERY COZY MYSTERY series, comprising six books (and counting); and of the CATS AND DOGS COZY MYSTERY series, comprising three books (and counting).

Fiona would love to hear from you, so please visit www.fionagraceauthor.com to receive free ebooks, hear the latest news, and stay in touch.

ISBN: 978-1-0943-7390-4

BOOKS BY FIONA GRACE

LACEY DOYLE COZY MYSTERY
MURDER IN THE MANOR (Book#1)
DEATH AND A DOG (Book #2)
CRIME IN THE CAFE (Book #3)
VEXED ON A VISIT (Book #4)
KILLED WITH A KISS (Book #5)
PERISHED BY A PAINTING (Book #6)
SILENCED BY A SPELL (Book #7)
FRAMED BY A FORGERY (Book #8)
CATASTROPHE IN A CLOISTER (Book #9)

TUSCAN VINEYARD COZY MYSTERY
AGED FOR MURDER (Book #1)
AGED FOR DEATH (Book #2)
AGED FOR MAYHEM (Book #3)
AGED FOR SEDUCTION (Book #4)
AGED FOR VENGEANCE (Book #5)
AGED FOR ACRIMONY (Book #6)

DUBIOUS WITCH COZY MYSTERY
SKEPTIC IN SALEM: AN EPISODE OF MURDER (Book #1)
SKEPTIC IN SALEM: AN EPISODE OF CRIME (Book #2)
SKEPTIC IN SALEM: AN EPISODE OF DEATH (Book #3)

BEACHFRONT BAKERY COZY MYSTERY
BEACHFRONT BAKERY: A KILLER CUPCAKE (Book #1)
BEACHFRONT BAKERY: A MURDEROUS MACARON (Book #2)
BEACHFRONT BAKERY: A PERILOUS CAKE POP (Book #3)
BEACHFRONT BAKERY: A DEADLY DANISH (Book #4)
BEACHFRONT BAKERY: A TREACHEROUS TART (Book #5)
BEACHFRONT BAKERY: A CALAMITOUS COOKIE (Book #6)

CATS AND DOGS COZY MYSTERY
A VILLA IN SICILY: OLIVE OIL AND MURDER (Book #1)
A VILLA IN SICILY: FIGS AND A CADAVER (Book #2)
A VILLA IN SICILY: VINO AND DEATH (Book #3)

CHAPTER ONE

Lacey rubbed her fatigued eyes and glanced down at her extensive to-do list.

Who knew a supposedly low-key wedding took so much planning?

So far, she'd decided on the theme—Rustic Romance—and a color palette of ivory and taupe. She'd picked the flowers—orchids, white roses, and dried hydrangeas—which Gina was now taking full ownership over. But whether she wanted gilded tableware, or burlap linens, or stain-finished banquet tables still eluded her.

"I swear my to-do list is breeding," she murmured to herself, tucking a dark curl behind her ear.

Of course, this wasn't her first time down the aisle. Indeed, it wasn't Tom's either. Because of their past histories, they'd both been very certain about not wanting an elaborate blowout this time around, and yet somehow there was still so much to decide. Decisions that would be infinitely more easy to make if Lacey addressed the elephant in the room, the unspoken question mark of her father.

She glanced over at the envelope she'd received from him, his RSVP to her wedding invite. Weeks had passed since it had arrived, and she'd not yet built up the courage to open it. Just as she had with every step along the way in her search for her missing father, Lacey's fear was her biggest roadblock. Learning the truth of his abandonment after all these years caused her more anxiety than her fantastical ruminations did—at least in her mind he could be a spy, rather than just a man who'd turned his back on his parental duties.

Ever since the letter arrived, Lacey had been telling herself she'd open it tomorrow. But she kept pushing tomorrow back and back. She couldn't stand the thought of him declining the invite and not being there to walk her down the aisle, missing a pivotal moment in her life just as he had her marriage to David.

So the envelope had remained unopened, waiting, just so Lacey could cling onto that small sliver of hope that it said he was coming.

Just then, Lacey heard a gentle knock on the door. She swiveled in her office chair. "Come in."

The door opened a few inches. A take-away coffee cup emerged through the gap.

"Pumpkin spiced latte?" came Gina's disembodied voice.

Lacey smiled at her friend's generosity. "Thank you!"

But in the next instant, she became suspicious. Gina only ever bought her things to butter her up.

"What have you done?" Lacey asked, directing her question to the coffee-cup-holding hand of Gina.

The door was pushed fully open to reveal the older woman. She was dressed in a long brown cotton dress and white apron, a lace-up bodice, and a white frilly bonnet perched on her gray hair. Pointy suede shoes poked out from beneath the folds of her skirt. She was in costume.

Lacey groaned. Halloween was fast approaching, and she'd never been particularly fond of the holiday. The town of Wilfordshire, England, where she lived, on the other hand, seemed absolutely obsessed with it. Gina in particular seemed to think it was the best thing since sliced bread. She hadn't stopped asking Lacey when she'd be allowed to dress up for work for weeks now. Lacey had felt like she'd been in a tug of war with a child rather than a sixty-odd-year-old woman.

"Gina, we've talked about this," Lacey told her best friend and employee.

"I know, I know!" Gina interjected before Lacey had a chance to say any more. "No costumes until Halloween. But the decorations are going up in the High Street, and everyone else in town is wearing one."

She paced inside the office and thrust the coffee cup under Lacey's nose, squinching her eyes to see if her apology latte would work.

Lacey narrowed her eyes. With defeat, she took the take-out coffee cup from Gina. The gorgeous smell of ginger wafted into her nostrils.

"So, what are you supposed to be?" she asked, scanning Gina's costume from head to toe. "Some kind of peasant woman?"

"I'm Violet Jourdemayne!" Gina exclaimed, as if the name ought to mean something to Lacey.

"Who?" Lacey asked.

Behind her red-framed spectacles, Gina's eyes widened. "Only the most famous witch of Wilfordshire!"

But before she had a chance to explain more, the office door suddenly swung all the way open. Boudica, Gina's English Shepherd dog, had nudged it open, and she came trotting in. She was wearing a pair of red devil horns on her head.

"Oh, Gina!" Lacey admonished.

"What?" Gina replied. "She loves dressing up, don't you, Boo?"

Boudica completed a proud lap around Lacey's small office like she was a pedigree at Crufts.

"Besides," Gina added, "I hoped once you saw Boudica's costume you'd be more inclined to let me keep mine." She grinned hopefully.

The devil horns belong on her, Lacey thought, ruefully. Her friend was using the same tactic Lacey's nephew back in New York City was so good at; pleading for forgiveness rather than asking for permission.

"I haven't exactly been given a choice," Lacey said. "I'm not going to send you home to change, am I?"

Gina hopped excitedly from foot to foot, looking triumphant. Lacey rolled her eyes lovingly.

"Great!" Gina exclaimed. "Because I got this for *you*." She handed Lacey a pair of black glasses affixed to an Albert Einstein wig. "And *these* for Chester!" She held out a pair of alien antennas.

"Now you're pushing it," Lacey said, switching into her boss persona to nip this in the bud. "I'm putting my foot down now. I draw the line. I'm not dressing up, and I won't have you dressing Chester up either. He's not a toy."

From her place at the door, Gina pouted. But Lacey nodded resolutely. She found it hard to act like the boss of her own business sometimes, especially when her main employee was her best friend, so she put her attention on the latte in order to avoid looking at Gina's forlorn expression. Spicy ginger danced across her taste buds.

"Trust my luck to move to the one town in the UK that takes Halloween more seriously than back home." She shuddered as she remembered all the gaudy Halloween parties she'd suffered through back in New York City, most of them at her sister's instigation; Naomi really had a skill for finding the tackiest of events.

"Wilfordshire had a lot of very famous witch trials," Gina explained. "More than any other town in England. The first executions were here."

"How awful."

"That's why it is such an important part of our history," Gina continued.

"So that's why you're dressed as a witch?" Lacey asked over the lip of her coffee. "As some kind of homage?"

Gina puffed herself up proudly. "Violet Jourdemayne is the most famous witch around these parts. She was accused of making kids sick and was hanged from an oak tree in a field in Ippledean. After her death, the kids continued to get sick, so the villagers figured she was haunting the tree and set it ablaze. Apparently it took a week to burn."

"Uh-huh…" Lacey said, not believing a word of the story, beyond the fact of some poor woman being scapegoated and executed.

Gina nodded eagerly. "Yes. And then from the ashes a magpie flew out. Violet's spirit lives on. Now, whenever you see a magpie in Ippledean, you have to cross yourself."

Lacey grimaced. Gina wasn't going to have much luck getting her to warm to the holiday with those kinds of morbid tales.

"You know…" Gina said, "all the other stores are putting up decorations."

Lacey sighed.

That's what happens when you give an inch, she thought.

"I don't think we should decorate," she told her employee. "All that tacky plastic stuff isn't exactly in keeping."

"I don't mean like that," Gina said. "I mean we need to get all the creepier items out on display. The china dolls, for example, should be front and center. And what about that battered rocking chair? And all those old leather-bound books? I could make quite a creepy window display if you'll let me."

"I don't want to lure people in thinking we're some kind of occult store," Lacey countered. "They might be disappointed once they realize it's all about antique teacups and vintage lamps."

Gina put a finger in the air to indicate she had already thought of this. "Which is precisely why you should do a stock trip to Ippledean this afternoon. There are plenty of secondhand stores there, you're bound to find some great oddities. Are you aware we don't have a single piece of taxidermy in the stock room?"

"For good reason," Lacey said with a shudder. "Taxidermy is gross."

"It's spooky," Gina countered. "And people like spooky things on Halloween."

Lacey considered it. She might not particularly like Halloween, but if others did, she'd be remiss not to cater to them. Besides, she had too much wedding planning to be getting on with to quibble with Gina over a window display.

"Fine," she said. "You can decorate."

Gina punched the air triumphantly. She'd gotten her way twice today, and the store hadn't even opened its doors to customers yet.

"But nothing gaudy," Lacey warned. "And I want it all taken down and everything put back to normal the minute it hits November. And if you put that alien thing on Chester's head, I'm firing you."

Gina nodded eagerly, clearly happy to accept the terms. Lacey tutted and shook her head affectionately as her friend hurried out of the office to get to work, her devil dog trotting out after her.

Finally alone again, Lacey swirled back to her to-do list. But as she did, she misjudged where she was placing her coffee cup. She dropped it, spilling scolding hot latte onto her jeans.

Lacey jumped out of her chair with a wince, knocking a stack of papers. They fell to the floor, fanning out across the carpet.

"That's just perfect," Lacey muttered.

She dumped the cup in the trash can, then set about rescuing the papers from the puddle of ginger latte. As she began picking them up, she spotted the envelope from her father scattered amongst them.

A wave of emotion washed through her, so powerful it overcame the pain of the hot coffee on her leg. She fell to her knees, grabbed the letter, and clutched it to her chest.

That was too close a call, she thought, as tears filled her eyes. If the letter had gotten ruined by coffee, she would've been furious with herself.

She removed the letter from her chest and peered at it through her misted eyes. It was the first time she'd really inspected it closely. It was curiously light, and her father's handwriting was shaky. She wondered if he'd been emotional as he'd written her name. It was the name he'd chosen for her, after all, one that he'd freely added to the bottom of every Christmas and birthday card for seven years until one day, he'd just walked out on the family. Had it moved him, writing the name of his eldest daughter once again, for the first time in decades? Or was the shaking in his handwriting due to age? He would be in his seventies now, after all. He may well have developed arthritis, like many people did as they got older.

Lacey's heart started to pound. The near miss with the coffee made it suddenly crystal clear that she could not keep putting off this moment. The longer she left it, the more likely it was that the letter would get damaged or lost or ruined. She had to open it now. It was time to learn the truth.

Her breath became ragged from anticipation and nerves. Before she got the chance to talk herself out of it, she grabbed the letter opener off the desk, flipped the envelope over, and sliced it open.

Then she took a deep breath and reached inside.

The envelope was empty.

Empty? Lacey thought with a frown. *What the heck?*

She didn't understand. What did it mean?

Crestfallen, she turned the envelope upside down and shook it, on the off chance her father had mailed her some kind of abstract clue, like a feather or a petal. But nothing fell from it.

Next she peered inside, checking to see whether anything had gotten caught in the corners or crevices. There was definitely nothing inside.

With bitter disappointment, Lacey realized her father had mailed her a blank envelope. After all that emotional build-up, she'd been left with nothing.

She sat back on the floor, perplexed and shell-shocked. Of all the millions of outcomes she'd imagined, this one had never crossed her mind.

All that investigative work, she thought with frustration. *For nothing!*

She couldn't help it—she felt betrayed by her father all over again.

In need of a supportive ear, Lacey pushed up from the floor and headed for the main shop in search of Gina. Perhaps the older woman would have some words of wisdom to comfort her in her moment of disappointment.

She paced along the corridor, holding the empty envelope in her hands, peering at it intently, as if perhaps she could will an answer into existence.

"Hey, Gina," she said, passing beneath the archway onto the main shop floor. "I need to talk to you."

She looked up expecting to see her friend, but froze, aghast, as a wholly horrifying sight awaited her…

Gina had completely covered the store in decorations.

Lacey's eyes widened with shock as she glanced from the tacky rubber skeletons dangling from the ceiling, to the big black spider silhouettes stuck to the inside of the windows.

There were so many decorations, the only way Gina would have been able to carry it off was if she'd started decorating the moment

Lacey had locked herself in her office this morning, long before she'd asked for permission.

That rascal! Lacey thought.

She slid the letter into the back pocket of her jeans and stalked across the shop floor.

"Gina!" she cried.

Chester, who'd been slumbering in his usual spot beside the counter, woke up, his eyebrows rising with interest. But other than waking up the dog, Lacey's yell was met by silence.

"Gina!" she tried again.

Chester lifted both ears quizzically.

"Have you seen her?" Lacey asked him.

Chester just tipped his head to the side cluelessly and let out a little whinny.

Lacey turned on the spot, narrowing her eyes as she peered in between the couches and armoires to see if she could spot her friend's frizzy gray hair poking out. She must've gone into hiding, Lacey reasoned, fearing her wrath for decorating the store so tackily.

"Where is she hiding?" Lacey muttered under her breath.

She paced toward Vintage Valley. Then, suddenly, she saw something that made her freeze.

A pair of shoes were poking out around the side of a bookcase.

Lacey gasped. But then she thought of all the tacky decorations Gina had filled the store with.

It's just a dummy... she thought.

Still, she stepped closer just in case.

But as she got closer, she realized with horror it was no dummy. Finnbar, the young shop assistant, was lying sprawled on the floor, on his back.

"Finnbar!" Lacey cried, rushing toward him. "What happened? Did you fall? Are you hurt?"

At that very moment, Gina emerged from the shadows.

"It—it was an accident!" she stammered.

That's when Lacey saw she was holding a bloodied knife.

7

CHAPTER TWO

Lacey's eyes widened with terror at the sight of the knife. Without meaning to, she let out a bloodcurdling scream. Tremors shook her body.

At the sound of her scream, Boudica and Chester began barking feverishly. They started running circles around Finnbar, pawing at his lifeless body.

Lacey looked desperately from Gina's bloodied knife to the boy on the ground, barely able to register what she was seeing. Gina and Finnbar butted heads at the best of times, but she'd had no idea it had gone this far.

"G—Gina," she stammered. "Wh—what did you do?"

Gina looked stunned, like she had no explanation for her actions. "I don't know. It was an accident."

"How do you stab someone accidentally?" Lacey cried incredulously.

Suddenly, Finnbar spluttered and sat up.

"He's still alive!" Lacey cried, snapping into action.

She tried to recall the first aid training she'd undertaken about a decade ago. Of course it was a good sign he was conscious, but things could change quickly when you were dealing with bleeding.

"Stay calm," she commanded him. "We need to stem the flow." She started searching his plaid shirt for the wound. "Gina! Don't just stand there! Call an ambulance!"

Finnbar was shaking, emitting a strange choking noise. Then Lacey realized something. He wasn't choking, he was chuckling.

She drew back, taking him by the shoulders and staring into his hazel eyes. He was laughing!

Lacey glowered over her shoulder to discover Gina bent over in hysterics.

It dawned on Lacey then that this whole thing was a set-up. A joke.

The adrenaline whooshed out of her. She sat back on her haunches, stunned. She couldn't believe they'd pull a practical joke on her like that. So much for butting heads. Her two employees had joined forces against her.

"I wish you could've seen her face," Gina said to Finnbar through her spluttering giggles.

"I'm so sorry I spoiled it," Finnbar replied. "It was Boudicca's fault. Her tail got in my mouth."

He patted the pup's head between the devil horns. The dog seemed to have calmed down from all the drama. Chester, too, had recovered from the scare.

No such luck for Lacey. Her nerves were shot.

"I can't believe you two," she huffed, her heart racing a mile a minute.

Pranks like that were just another reason why she hated Halloween. The line between funny and cruel was far too easily crossed, in her opinion.

"We got her good, huh?" Gina said to Finnbar, holding her hand down to help him up.

Finnbar, clearly misunderstanding the gesture, gave her a high five instead.

"Laugh it up, guys," Lacey said as she stood and dusted herself down. "Just remember I'm the one who decides your Christmas bonuses."

Their laughter stopped instantly. Their expressions fell. They exchanged guilty, ashamed looks with one another.

Lacey turned away to hide the smirk on her lips. Of course she had no intention of depriving her hardworking employees of their Christmas bonuses, but if they were going to play pranks on her, then she'd play pranks on them in return!

Just then, the bell over the door jangled, ushering in the first customer of the day. Lacey skipped off to attend to him, leaving her misbehaving employees to think about their actions, and to believe they'd brought quite a hefty punishment upon themselves.

The customer who'd entered was a funny-looking man, dressed in a scratchy-looking pair of brown chaps and a mustard-colored tweed jacket. Along with his mutton chops, it looked as if he'd just stepped through a time portal and ended up here from the Victorian era.

At first, Lacey presumed he was in costume. The Demon Barber of Fleet Street perhaps? But as she got a little closer, she realized his mutton chops were very much real, and she was left wondering if this was just how he usually chose to dress.

"Good morning," she said, brightly. "Can I help you?"

The man gave barely a cursory glance at Finnbar sitting on the floor, or Gina, dressed as a medieval witch holding a fake bloody knife. He didn't even seem to register the two English Shepherd dogs fussing around his legs, one of whom was wearing devil horns. He simply announced, in a very posh accent, "I am seeking some taxidermy."

Out of the corner of her eye, Lacey saw Gina flash her a knowing *I-told-you-so* look, but chose to ignore her, because she was still mad about the prank and wasn't ready to give her a win.

"I'm afraid we don't have any taxidermy," Lacey told the odd man. "But we do have some spooky items over here for the holiday."

She led him to the small area of peculiar items Gina had cobbled together on a round chestnut dining table covered with lace cloth. There wasn't very much available; an old Victorian optometrist's set, a bunch of spooky-looking China dolls, and a bronze telescope.

The man removed a monocle from his top pocket and peered at the small range of items on display. Then he shook his head and straightened up.

"No, that's not really what I'm after," he said. "Maybe an insect in resin, or a preserved rodent in a jar would do, but none of these are remotely suitable for my needs."

All Lacey could do was blink. She was tempted to ask what on earth he might need a preserved insect, pickled rodent, or stuffed animal for, but decided on second thought she'd prefer not to know.

"I shall head to Ippledean!" the strange man announced. "They're bound to have something there."

And with that, he strode away, the bronze store bell tinkling above him as he left.

The whole encounter was truly bizarre. But it made something clear in Lacey's mind.

She returned to her employees—Finnbar now wearing the rejected Einstein glasses and wig combo—and held her hands up in a truce.

"I guess you guys win," she said. "People really do want Halloween things. In which case, I'd better give them Halloween things." If she was going to have to suffer through the holiday, she may as well capitalize on it. "How do you two feel about a spooky-themed auction?"

Finnbar and Gina exchanged a reticent look.

"I know what you're thinking," Lacey continued. "It'll take a lot of work to get organized in time, so I'll need all hands on deck. Stock. Website. Posters. Everything."

"Will we get our Christmas bonuses back?" Finnbar asked.

"Absolutely," Lacey told him.

"And will you wear a costume?" Gina asked.

"If I must," Lacey replied.

Her two employees looked at one another again, then finally nodded their agreement.

"Excellent," Lacey said. "It's settled."

Her burlap linen and gilded kitchenware decision could wait. She was feeling suddenly very motivated to plan an auction instead of a wedding.

"First things first," she announced. "I'm going to do a stock run to Ippledean. It seems like that's the place to go for all things spooky. Can I trust you two to mind the store for the day without breaking anything or killing one another?"

"Yes," Finnbar said, his pale cheeks growing pink at the reminder of their prank.

Lacey looked expectantly at Gina.

Gina nodded. "I promise."

"Good," Lacey said.

She collected her car keys off the counter and whistled for Chester. He came trotting to her and they headed for the exit.

"Oh, Lacey," Gina called. "You might want to change first."

She pointed at Lacey's leg.

Lacey glanced down. The coffee she'd spilled earlier had stained her jeans. But there wasn't much she could do about it now.

She shrugged. "I'll just tell people I'm dressed as a hobo for Halloween."

Just then, she remembered the envelope she'd stashed in her back pocket. She was about to bring it up when she was once again distracted. Not by the sight of her injured assistant this time, but by something altogether more bizarre outside her window.

It appeared that a huge oak tree was slowly moving along the High Street...

The large ten-foot tree bobbed up and down as it slowly moved across the cobblestones. Then it halted right outside her door.

"What now?" Lacey exclaimed.

There was always something going on!

She hurried out of the store to see what bizarre thing the town was up to now.

CHAPTER THREE

The chill of fall was in the air as Lacey exited the store, Chester in tow.

Wilfordshire's High Street was made up of old stone terraced stores, with bay-style windows that bulged out into the streets. Bunting crisscrossed from one side to the next, strung between the Victorian-style lamp posts, and it was currently Halloween themed in orange and black. The streets were bustling with kids and adults alike all dressed in costumes, flowing around the large oak tree that had suddenly appeared right in the middle of their path. And, more importantly, right in front of Lacey's store entrance!

The eccentricities of Wilfordshire often perplexed Lacey, but this one really was the most bizarre she'd ever witnessed.

With Chester trotting alongside her, Lacey marched across the cobblestones over to the large oak tree. It seemed for once she was not alone in her confusion. The sudden intrusion of the enormous tree had also prompted Taryn, the boutique owner from next door, outside as well. Though the two women famously didn't get along, it appeared on this one matter they saw eye-to-eye.

"What is this thing?" Taryn mused.

"Beats me," Lacey murmured in reply.

They both marched toward the intruding oak tree with matching scowls.

Taryn wasn't wearing a costume, Lacey noted, and was in her normal black dress and heels combo. The asymmetrical dark bobbed hair cut she'd copied off Lacey at the beginning of the year was now down to her shoulders—the exact same length Lacey was currently wearing hers, incidentally. Taryn had been copying her hair ever since Lacey had started a relationship with Taryn's ex-beau Tom, as if that might be enough to win him back.

Taryn's heels clip-clip-clipped like a marching drum as they advanced in unison. As they got closer, Lacey saw the enormous tree was actually a float on wheels, like the type one might see in a parade. It had been rather intricately crafted, and was actually quite beautifully designed. Which of course did not mitigate the problem of it being suddenly parked outside her store!

"Hello?" Lacey asked, peering around the large tree in search of its owner. "What's going on here?"

"How on earth is anyone going to see my amazing black lace couture window display with that thing in the way?" Taryn added, antagonistically, folding her arms across her bony, concave chest.

Of course she would approach the situation all guns blazing, rather than Lacey's slightly more gentle approach.

"Is that you, Lacey?" a female voice said from the other side of the tree's thick trunk.

Suddenly, a face suddenly popped around. It took Lacey a moment to recognize Lucia, the manager of the Lodge, because she'd dyed her hair a vibrant red color, and was wearing a dress made up of patchwork fabric held together with safety pins. She, like everyone else, seemed to be getting into the spirit of Halloween.

"It is you," Lucia said. Her face looked red from the exertion of dragging a ten-foot parade float through the cobblestone streets.

Lacey gestured to the tree. "What's this?"

"It's a Violet Jourdemayne effigy," Lucia explained.

She beckoned with her hand, and Lacey went around to the other side of the tree, where a ghostly female figure had been painted onto the bark, and a magpie painted into its branches. The work was so real, with fantastic shading and thin lines. At first glance, Lacey actually believed the witch was real, and she shivered as chills went up her spine.

Lacey was thoroughly impressed. She knew Lucia was creative from her time working at Tom's patisserie, but she'd had no idea she was *that* talented!

"You made this yourself?" she asked.

"I did," Lucia said. She beamed with pride, her smile stretching from ear to ear.

"It's really impressive," Lacey said. "But won't you be sad to burn it?"

She was a little mystified by the whole thing. It seemed like an awful waste to burn something so beautiful.

"Not really," Lucia replied. Far from looking unhappy to be setting fire to her stunning artwork, she looked proud. "It's an important part of Violet Jourdemayne's story. You know about our most famous witch, right?"

14

"Gina filled me in," Lacey replied, shuddering at the macabre story and the significance of this large tree effigy.

"We're burning it as the grand finale at the Halloween party at the Lodge," Lucia explained.

Taryn, who'd remained stony-faced throughout the whole exchange, suddenly interjected. "Never mind that. What's it doing here? In the street? Blocking my fabulous window display?"

Meekly, Lucia held up the rope with which she was pulling the float. "The bus wouldn't let me on with it, so I have to drag it to the Lodge myself. I'm just taking a little break. It's heavy." She glanced from one woman to the next. "Are you guys coming to the party?"

"I wouldn't come if you paid me," Taryn replied, haughtily, without missing a beat. "Make sure that thing's gone in five minutes, or I'll call the wardens and get you a parking ticket."

She marched away.

Lucia blinked, looking hurt. It was clear she wasn't used to Taryn's antics in the way Lacey was.

"Don't worry about her," Lacey told her. "She's always that mean."

She considered Lucia's invitation to the Halloween party at the Lodge. It was being put on by her good friend Suzy, and while Lacey obviously wanted to support her, she also really didn't enjoy costume parties. Unless they were with her eight-year-old nephew, Frankie, and all his adorable friends, she personally didn't get much out of them. Like most people, she'd grown out of playing dress-up in her youth. But she'd never grown back into it during her college years as most of her peers had; she'd been far too focused on getting good grades to go to boozy costume parties. Now she cringed a little inside whenever attending an adults' fancy dress party.

Suddenly, Lacey remembered her plan to host a Halloween-themed auction, and an idea popped into her head. There *was* a way she could support Suzy while also making the whole dressing up thing a little more palatable for her personally.

"I'm holding a Halloween-themed auction this weekend," she told Lucia. "Would you guys mind if I put some flyers and posters up at the Lodge during the party?"

It was common practice for the two friends to advertise one another's businesses—Lacey always had a little stack of flyers for the Lodge beside her till, and Suzy had a whole table in the reception area of the Lodge devoted to advertising local Wilfordshire businesses. A

15

little push for an on-theme auction during the bash seemed like a decent enough idea.

"Of course," Lucia said, using her managerial authority. "We'll already have a bunch up from the ghost tour operator. The more the merrier."

"Great," Lacey said. "Then I'll see you there."

Just then, Lacey's phone started to ring. She grabbed it. Her mom was calling from back home in New York City.

Ever since Lacey had told her mom she could have more input into the wedding preparations, Shirley had been calling all hours of the night and day with suggestions. She was trying to be helpful, but Lacey was starting to find it quite annoying. Not that she'd ever tell Shirley that.

"I'd better take this," Lacey told Lucia. "Good luck getting that to the Lodge!"

"Thanks," Lucia said, turning her attention back to the tree with a look of determination.

Lacey headed off toward the side street where her car was parked, Chester trotting alongside her, and answered the call as she went.

"I've had a great idea for the wedding," Shirley announced the moment the call connected.

"Oh, right?" Lacey said, trying to keep her tone as light as possible, despite the inevitable spike in anxiety she felt whenever she was talking to her highly strung mother.

"Yes," Shirley continued. "Since it's set in the winter, why don't you have a big sleigh for people to put their gifts in?"

Lacey grimaced. She adopted a forced pleasant tone. "That's a fun idea. But Tom and I have decided not to have gifts. We're going to set up a donation page for Alice instead."

Lacey had recently become a donor for a donkey sanctuary, a gift her friends had organized for her fortieth birthday. Her adopted donkey was named Alice.

"You want your wedding donations to go to a donkey?" came Shirley's nonplussed reply.

"It doesn't go to her specifically," Lacey said. "It's shared out between her and all her donkey friends."

Shirley sighed. "Fine. If you say so. But please just have Santa in there somewhere for the kids. Or an elf? Ooh, you could hire reindeer! Perhaps your donkey friend knows some..."

"I'll think about it," Lacey said, humoring her.

16

There would of course be no Santas, sleighs, or elves anywhere near her wedding. Reindeer on the other hand... While that did somewhat interest an animal lover like herself, she wasn't sure Tom would be persuaded. She'd have to ask him at their dinner date tonight.

"Anyway, Mom," she said, as she reached her car and unlocked it, "thanks for all your ideas. I'll add them to the list. Speak later, okay?"

Chester jumped up into the Volvo and plonked himself firmly in the driver's seat. Lacey shooed him over with her hands but he refused to budge.

"You're going already?" came Shirley's incredulous voice from her cell phone as Lacey wedged it between her shoulder and ear in order to give Chester a nudge. "Where are you rushing off to now?"

"Halloween's coming up," Lacey explained, as her dog finally moved his furry backside over to the passenger seat, allowing Lacey to slide in after him. "Turns out everyone in this town goes gaga for it. So I'm stocking up on creepy things for an auction..."

Her voice trailed away as she spotted the coffee stain on her legs and was reminded of the letter from her father. She'd been so distracted by Gina and Finnbar's horrible prank, and the odd man searching for taxidermy, and the sudden appearance of a big oak tree outside her store, she'd completely forgotten about it.

She was hit by a sudden urge to talk to her mom about it. But she held back. Shirley was never able to stay impartial on matters pertaining to her ex-husband. It was near impossible for Shirley to keep the scathing tone from her voice when discussing him, and no matter how true or justified her criticisms of him might be, he was Lacey's dad first and foremost and she simply didn't want to hear it.

"How dreadful," Shirley was saying, in response to her creepy auction announcement. "Whatever you do, don't buy a Ouija board. It's not sensible to mess with the occult, even if it is all ludicrous nonsense. No tarot cards. None of that mystical stuff. Just stick to the usual bats and gargoyles."

Their dislike of Halloween might be one of the few things mother and daughter shared.

"Don't worry, Mom," Lacey replied. "I have no intentions of messing with the occult."

"Good," Shirley said. "I'll call you later to discuss table runners. I know you said taupe and ivory for the color scheme, but I've seen the most amazing gold-trimmed ones."

"You can tell me all about it later," Lacey said.

She ended the call and looked over at Chester beside her.

"Your grandmother thinks we should have reindeer at the wedding," she told him, starting the ignition. "What do you think about that?"

He wagged his tail excitedly and barked.

"My thoughts exactly," Lacey said. "You'd find them far too interesting, and you and Boudicca would get distracted trying to herd them and forget all about your bridesmaid and groomsman duties."

She petted him under the chin affectionately, and was about to head off on her journey to Ippledean when her phone rang again.

"If that's her calling back..." Lacey muttered between her teeth.

Shirley wasn't very good at accepting that Lacey had other things to be getting on with. If she was calling back with some ridiculous idea like a fifty-foot Christmas tree or an ice rink, Lacey wasn't sure how levelheaded she'd be able to remain.

But when she checked her cell, the number was unrecognized.

Lacey frowned, wondering who might be calling her, and Chester barked to alert her to the fact her phone was still ringing in her hand.

Lacey answered. The sound of a very plummy man filled her ear.

"I'm calling from Knightsbridge Auction House," he said. "I have been given your contact details from a gentleman named Percy Johnson."

"Yes, I know Percy," Lacey replied.

The kindly old antiquarian had become something of a mentor to Lacey when she first started her business venture. She was very fond of him. He had a wonderful grandfatherly energy that always put Lacey at ease.

She was suddenly struck with a fear that something might have happened to him. "Is he okay?"

"Why yes, he's perfectly well," the man replied. "The reason I'm calling is because we have a vacancy for an auctioneer. We approached Percy, but he declined and put your name forward instead, along with a very glowing recommendation indeed. We'd like to offer you a job."

CHAPTER FOUR

Lacey's hand tightened around her cell phone with astonishment. A job offer? At one of the most revered auction houses in London? She was almost too stunned to speak.

"I—I'm taken aback," Lacey said. "I don't know what to say."

"Shall I post you the details of the position?" came the plummy man's voice in her ear. "Salary, hours, and the like? I have your address as Crag Cottage in Wilfordshire. Is that right?"

"Y—yes, that's right," Lacey confirmed.

"Wonderful. Do take your time thinking it through. We shan't be holding interviews for at least two more weeks. I look forward to hearing your answer. Tatty-bye!"

"O—okay," Lacey said. "Thank you."

The brief call ended. In the mere minute it had taken, it had set Lacey into a total tailspin about her life and future.

She hadn't given much thought to her long-term plans. She was happy in Wilfordshire. She had a wedding coming up, a thriving business, a home, friends, a dog. A whole life. But was this where she stopped? Did that just mean this was her life now, forever? Or were there more opportunities for her on the horizon?

Outside the window of her car, she spotted a young woman leading a little clan of children dressed as ghosts across the street, hand in hand. A maternal urge stirred in Lacey's chest. She watched them in the rearview mirror until they disappeared around the corner.

"What is in the future?" she asked Chester.

In the passenger seat, her pup yipped his reply.

Lacey revved her rust-bucket secondhand car to life, and drove the short way to the neighboring town of Ippledean.

The weather turned a little grisly as the car puttered up the steep hills to the town's border. There was a church at the highest point, something Lacey had noticed seemed to be customary in old English towns. The church's bell tower doubled up as a viewing post; now open to the public as a tourist attraction, but likely used in the past to keep a watchful eye on all the streets, houses, and townsfolk below, as they went about their farming work in the marshy fields filled with grazing sheep.

"Well, isn't this charming?" Lacey said to Chester. She drove down the bumpy cobblestone road toward the medieval town center. "It looks like something from a storybook."

Chester barked his acknowledgment, watching out the window with interest at the tiny black timber-framed houses they passed, with their pitched roofs and Hobbit-sized wooden front doors.

Despite being a quaint place, with the same cobblestone streets as Wilfordshire, Ippledean's gruesome history became very apparent the moment Lacey reached the town center and happened upon a large grassy commons. Right in the middle of it was a stone statue of a gallows, a commemoration to three elderly women who'd been hanged on the spot for "conversing with the devil" centuries ago, though their odd behavior had since been re-attributed to dementia.

Many of the pubs had themed names, too. Lacey drove past the Three Witches, the Burning Oak, and the Hangman's Noose.

It was all a bit gruesome, and Lacey felt slightly on edge as she parked in a small gravel lot and headed to the shopping streets with Chester.

She quickly got lost in the maze of tiny roads. There was an abundance of independent stores—cute boutiques, jewelry shops, and a fair share of flea markets. But none of them appeared to be selling the types of macabre oddities Lacey had been led to believe Ippledean had to offer.

That was until she spotted a very narrow, dark alley in between two very closely positioned stores. It would have been very easily missed, had Lacey not been focusing so intently on the window display of a children's clothes store with cute little Halloween onesies in the window.

Feeling adventurous, Lacey decided to follow the narrow alleyway.

The buildings either side were so close together there was barely enough room for two people to pass side by side. Luckily, it was also very quiet here, in stark contrast to the bustling market area she'd just left.

It didn't take Lacey long to realize she'd stumbled upon the place where Ippledean's more unusual stores were tucked away out of sight. Among them she found an art store selling strange abstract murals, a brimming plant store with steamy windows, and a clothes shop that seemed to specialize in PVC catsuits.

Then Lacey spotted a very interesting window display up ahead. A beautiful ram's skull was in pride of place, next to an old typewriter and a battered accordion. It was the sort of window display Gina would love to recreate at the antiques store.

"This looks promising," Lacey told Chester.

The sign above the door read *The Ducking Stool*. Lacey headed inside.

The smell of dust wafted into Lacey's nostrils as she surveyed the gloomy store. There was very little artificial light, just a couple of yellow bulbs hanging from the ceiling, and not much daylight streaming in through the small curb-side window. It had a very creepy vibe that made prickles go up and down Lacey's spine. Chester clearly felt uncomfortable in this environment too because his fur was standing on end.

Just then, Lacey noticed a large counter to one side, behind which sat a bored-looking goth girl with lots of metal in her face. She had her nose in a large book.

The girl neither looked up nor greeted Lacey. In fact, she didn't bother to even acknowledge she was there. Lacey took that to mean she had free rein to peruse at her leisure, and headed for the shelves.

To her surprise, she quickly realized the store wasn't actually an antiques store at all, as she'd guessed it to be from the window display. It was in fact a pawn shop, but none like Lacey had ever seen before. Rather than the standard acoustic guitars and computer games she'd expect to see in the average pawn store, this one was full of bizarre and esoteric items.

Lacey quickly found four Victorian apothecary bottles, the type used by pharmacists to store pills (or poison) in amber- and blue-colored glass. They were on sale for twenty pounds for the lot, though Lacey immediately knew they were worth at least that much each. She felt a little thrill of excitement that she'd found her first auction item.

She carried the bottles over to the counter.

"Can I leave these here while I keep looking?" she asked the clerk.

The goth girl's eyes barely flicked up from her novel. She grunted apathetically. Lacey took that as a yes and continued scouting for treasure.

Next, she happened upon several blocks of insects in resin—scorpions, beetles, giant centipedes. Each one was labeled as a "paperweight," though Lacey could tell they weren't made from acrylic resin like the types easily found online. These were proper Victorian collectibles, probably from a museum. The Victorians had been absolutely obsessed with the natural world, cataloguing and stuffing every species they could get their hands on. Though each insect block was on sale for five pounds, Lacey was confident she'd be able to sell each one on for fifty.

She felt elated as she carried the collection over to the counter and placed them alongside her chemists' bottles.

"Your store is a treasure trove!" she commented to the goth girl.

The girl merely blinked at her through her kohl-rimmed eyes.

Trying not to pay too much mind to the girl, Lacey continued her hunt. She was starting to feel quite excited by what she might find, and headed to the back portion of the store.

She was not disappointed. Here, she found a whole range of taxidermy animals—a tortoise, an owl, and a red squirrel—in glass display boxes.

"Jackpot," she told Chester.

Her dog was staring at the squirrel in particular with a peculiar expression. Chester loved chasing squirrels up trees, and was clearly perplexed as to why this one was completely motionless … and dressed in clothes.

"I wonder what kind of people live in Ippledean," Lacey whispered to her sidekick dog as she retrieved the squirrel from the shelf. "If they have taxidermy to pawn off…"

Chester followed alongside her as she carried the three stuffed animals to the counter and placed them alongside the rest of her macabre findings.

"I'll be taking the ram's skull in the window too," she told the clerk. "If you don't mind fetching it for me."

The girl shot Lacey a daggered look, as if her request was the biggest inconvenience in the world. She dumped her book down loudly on the countertop and clomped over to the window in chunky black boots.

What a charming young woman, Lacey thought sarcastically, before heading off in search of more treasure.

As she scoured every inch of the shop, Lacey thought about the job offer she'd just received. If she worked for someone else, she'd never be able to put on her own themed auctions again. She'd never be able to go on her exploratory stock trips around England with Chester. If she sold someone else's goods, she'd lose all agency. She was quite certain that she'd be turning down the job offer from Knightsbridge Auction

House, but she at the very least wanted to check the job specification when it arrived in the mail. Maybe once she saw how much salary they were offering, it might be a different story.

Suddenly, Lacey felt eyes on her. A prickle went up her spine. She glanced over toward a shadowy corner of the store. Two large, round eyes were fixed on her.

Lacey leapt out of her skin, her heart racing in her chest. Then she realized what it was staring at her—a ventriloquist's dummy in a three-piece suit. She let out a nervous giggle.

"I think we've found our next item," she said to Chester.

If a toy could make her jump out of her skin, then it definitely deserved a place in her spooky auction.

She headed over to the shadowy corner to collect the ugly wooden dummy. But as she rounded the shelving unit protruding part way into the corridor, she discovered the best find of the day.

An entire anatomical teaching aid skeleton.

It would make the perfect addition to her auction, and Lacey leaned in closer to inspect it.

"It's real," she told Chester, shuddering.

Her gaze fell to the label. The pawn shop was selling it for two hundred pounds. But with Lacey's skilled auctioneering techniques, she hoped she'd be able to sell it on for closer to five.

She tucked the dummy under one arm and took hold of the bronze pole the skeleton was affixed to, wheeling it across the shop floor beside her over to the counter. Chester could hardly contain himself as he skipped and raced around it in circles. If a frozen squirrel had perplexed him, a life-sized skeleton on wheels had blown his little doggy mind.

"That's everything," Lacey said to the store clerk, bringing the skeleton to a stop beside the counter. "I've searched every nook of the place."

The bored goth girl had fetched the ram's skull for her from the window and laid it out beside the rest of her finds. It was exciting seeing them all together, and Lacey began imagining them displayed for her audience at the auction. She was confident she'd be able to use her flourishing auctioneering skills to turn a profit. Perhaps she should buy some crushed black velvet to display them on?

The girl began silently ringing up Lacey's purchases. It was quite uncomfortable, Lacey thought, standing there in silence with nothing but the beep-beep-beep of the till as the girl keyed in each price.

23

"I'm an auctioneer," she explained, in an attempt to ease her discomfort. "I'm holding a Halloween-themed auction. In Wilfordshire. Everyone loves Halloween there, with the witch trials and all. Violet Jourdemayne. You know the one?"

The girl looked at her through her black-rimmed eyes, blinked slowly, then returned to ringing up her purchases. She clearly didn't care one jot about what Lacey was saying.

Feeling even more awkward now with a failed interaction under her belt, Lacey rocked back on her heels, whistling to fill the silence. She glanced about, looking everywhere but at the girl.

As her gaze roved around, Lacey noticed a book on a disorganized and cluttered shelving unit behind the counter. She guessed it was a storage shelf, either full of items not yet displayed or items that had been bought and subsequently returned. The book that had caught her attention looked absolutely ancient, with dog-eared pages and a thick, battered leather spine. There appeared to be some strange shapes etched onto the front cover. Symbols? Or runes?

"Can I take a look at that?" Lacey asked the clerk, her intrigue getting the better of her.

The bored girl looked over her shoulder to see what Lacey was pointing at.

"The book?" she said.

It was the first time she'd spoken and Lacey almost fell over with surprise. "Yes, please. If I may."

The girl shrugged and lifted the book from the shelf, carelessly knocking over a bunch of other things as she did and making absolutely no attempt to tidy the mess. She handed the book lazily across the counter to Lacey.

It was weighty, far heavier than Lacey had anticipated, and the leather binding smelled strongly of hide.

Beside her, Chester let out a low growl.

"It gives you the heebie-jeebies too, huh?" Lacey asked him.

He barked shrilly. The goth girl glared at him.

"Shhh," Lacey soothed her pup.

She began to flip through the pages. They were thick, almost greasy to the touch, and yellow-brown in color. Some were curled, others dog-eared, others torn out altogether.

The book appeared to be written in an old language, like Latin or Gaelic, and between the chunks of text were pictures drawn in black ink of strange occult symbols.

Lacey had no idea what she was holding, but she felt very strongly drawn to it.

Her antique knowledge told her that most old texts didn't fetch nearly as much during resale as one might expect something that had survived hundreds of years of the annals of time to. A decent book of sufficient rarity could indeed fetch hundreds of dollars, sometimes thousands, but there was no way for Lacey to know what exactly this kind of book was. It may very well be worthless, but it fit with Lacey's auction theme so perfectly she was willing to take a risk on it.

"I'll take the book, too," she told the clerk, handing it back over.

As the girl took it from her, Chester barked again, very loudly. The goth girl shot him a piercing glare.

"Sorry, he's not usually like this," Lacey said.

She turned her attention to her dog, crouching down to comfort him.

"It's just a silly old book," she told him soothingly. "It won't do you any harm."

Chester's barks died down to a low grumble. Ever since she'd picked up that book, his curiosity and excitement had disappeared. Now he seemed very on edge.

Lacey suddenly remembered her mom's warning from earlier. *Don't mess with the occult.*

Her stomach turned. Was she making a decision she'd later come to regret?

CHAPTER FIVE

"There's no price on it," came a voice from above Lacey.

Lacey straightened up and faced the Ducking Stool's clerk. The young goth woman was holding the book in her hands, turning it over as she searched for a tag.

She gave up with a shrug. "I guess you can just take it."

Lacey shook her head. Though she didn't have the time or specific expertise to value the book on the spot, she simply wasn't willing to accept it for nothing.

"Add twenty pounds for it," she suggested.

She suspected she was lowballing here, but it was still twenty pounds more than the girl was originally going to get for it.

The goth shrugged apathetically and added an extra twenty pounds as she continued ringing up the oddities on the till.

Just then, Lacey heard her phone go in her pocket.

"Excuse me one moment," she said, stepping away.

She checked her cell phone to see the contact flashing at her: *fiancé.* She'd renamed Tom in her phone after their engagement, and now she smiled to herself, as she did every time he called. Tom had gotten into the adorable habit of calling her every time he had an idea for the wedding.

Lacey felt a surge of warmth go through her as she answered the call. "Yes, my dear?"

"How do you feel about bread pudding?" Tom asked.

Lacey frowned. "For the wedding?"

It was a bizarre suggestion. A Shirley-level bizarre suggestion.

On the other end of the line, Tom barked out a laugh. "No, for tonight! I'm in the store now picking stuff up for our dinner date."

Lacey's eyes widened. She'd completely forgotten about their dinner date tonight!

She checked her watch. She only had thirty minutes to pack all this stuff into her car and get home!

"Er, bread pudding, sure, sounds perfect," she said rapidly, suddenly in a fluster.

"Great," came Tom's carefree response. "See you shortly, my love."

The call ended, and Lacey hurried back to the counter.

"How much do I owe you?" she asked the clerk in a rapid voice.

"Three hundred pounds," the girl replied.

Lacey thrust over the cash, scooped up her bizarre purchases, and staggered away, dragging the skeleton on a pole after her.

*

Tom was waiting on the doorstep of Crag Cottage as Lacey turned her Volvo into the driveway. The car's headlights illuminated his dark blond hair. His tanned arms were wrapped around a large brown paper grocery bag.

Immediately flustered for having kept him waiting, Lacey parked and jumped out of the car. Chester pushed past her and dashed up the pathway, jumping at Tom and pawing his camel-brown sweater.

Tom shoved the bag into one arm to free up the other so he could return Chester's enthusiastic greeting with a vigorous head scratch.

"I'm so sorry I'm late!" Lacey exclaimed as she hurried up the path and awkwardly leaned over Chester to bestow a peck on Tom's cheek.

"No problem," Tom said, accepting her kiss and the proceeding lick that came from the dog. "I only just got here." His gaze went over her shoulder and he frowned. "Is there someone sitting in your backseat?"

As Lacey hurriedly rummaged in her purse for her Rapunzel key, she peered over her shoulder to look at her car. The silhouette of the skeleton was visible in the moonlight, looking rather eerie in its upright position in her backseat. It had been the only way for Lacey to fit all her auction purchases into the car, with the skeleton seat-belted in the back seat like a passenger.

"Oh, that's just a skeleton," she said, shoving the door with her shoulder and staggering inside as it yielded.

Tom gave a final disconcerted look at the skeleton before stepping in after her.

"Do I need to ask *why* you have a skeleton in your car?" he asked as he followed her along the low-ceilinged corridor and into the kitchen.

Lacey hit the switch and the room flooded with bright, warm light.

"I'm holding an auction for Halloween," she said.

Tom placed his brown paper grocery bag on the wooden countertop and turned to face her with a frown.

27

"You are?" He sounded surprised. "What happened to 'I hate Halloween'?"

Lacey chuckled. She fetched a bottle of red wine from the rack, a Shiraz that gave her autumnal vibes.

"Well, I figured if you can't beat them, you join them," she said, setting it down on the side.

She poured them both a glass, then handed Tom his.

"Cheers," she said, finally breathing out a sigh of relief.

"Cheers," he replied, flashing her a loving smile.

Lacey sipped from her glass. The South African Shiraz she'd chosen was smooth and mellow. Exactly what she'd been hankering for.

As Tom began collecting bowls and utensils, Lacey peeped inside the grocery bag. Among the packs of flour and sugar she spotted a little paper bag filled with delicious-looking shiny red berries.

"What are these?" she asked, taking the bag out.

Tom peered back out of the cupboard he was busy rummaging in to see what she was talking about. "Cranberries," he said, before dipping his head back inside the cupboard.

"Cranberries in bread pudding?" Lacey asked.

"Yeah!" came Tom's enthusiastic exclamation from inside the cupboard. "Fresh cranberries in place of raisins makes bread pudding much more decadent."

Trust Tom to spruce up the recipe.

He emerged from the cupboard with what he'd been searching for—a large ceramic mixing bowl. It was an antique Lacey had picked up in London and became instantly too attached to, to sell. Lucky thing too. According to Tom, it was the best baking ware known to man.

"Pass the cranberries," he said.

Lacey passed the bag over and watched as Tom got to work. He whisked the cream, egg yolks, and canned pumpkin—an ingredient that had proven more difficult for Lacey to source than Victorian-era taxidermy.

"Can you believe they sell canned pumpkin in the 'world food' aisle?" Lacey said, turning the can in her hands. "Back home, this stuff is everywhere."

"We don't have the same history with pumpkins as you guys," Tom said, only half listening since his attention was taken up by his task.

"Not even at Halloween?"

"Nope. When I was growing up, you'd be lucky to find a store selling a pumpkin to carve, and there were none of those pick your own pumpkin patch things they have everywhere now. Turnips, on the other hand…"

Lacey laughed.

She always enjoyed cooking with Tom. She hadn't realized how very much in need of relaxing she truly was, of just spending some downtime with her fiancé doing something that wasn't wedding planning or stressing out about her father. She was grateful for a reprieve from the thoughts that had been swirling in her mind all day.

She rested her backside against the counter, wine glass in hand.

"I know I'm not a bread pudding expert," she said, "but what do we need pumpkin for anyway? It's a bit of a twist, isn't it, adding pureed pumpkin?"

Tom wiggled his chestnut brown brows. His green eyes sparked. "You know me. Why do something simply, when you can overcomplicate it?"

Lacey smiled. She sipped from her wine glass, admiring her handsome fiancé as he worked his culinary magic. It always pleased her, the way Tom's body moved while he cooked, like he was performing some kind of intricate dance. She delighted in every moment of it; the way he habitually pushed the sleeves of his shirt above his elbows, exposing his tanned forearms; the way he flicked his head any time his shaggy hair fell into his eyes; the way he handled his ingredients with such care and consideration.

He'd make a very good TV chef, Lacey decided. *The type that makes all the ladies swoon.*

As she envisioned Tom's future career as a TV chef, Lacey suddenly remembered the job offer she'd received from Knightsbridge Auction House. She'd barely thought about it all day, or given herself the chance to daydream about the different life she could live if she accepted the offer. Now she was at home with her fiancé, it seemed like a good idea to actually discuss it.

"Could you ever see yourself living in London?" she asked, trying to gauge his response first.

"Absolutely not," Tom replied without taking even a second to consider it. "It's far too busy. Way too expensive. And there's so much pollution. Not to mention commuting to work on the Tube every day. I think I'd go mad if I lived in London."

That wasn't a good start.

"Well, I got a job offer today," she announced. "In London."

Tom's face snapped to her, his eyebrows raised. Lacey knew she'd shocked him, because he'd actually turned his attention away from his food preparations.

"Oh?" he asked.

Lacey ran her fingertips along the rim of her wine glass hesitantly. "Yes. From Knightsbridge Auction House in London."

Tom coughed, choking on nothing but his astonishment. "Knightsbridge?"

Lacey nodded. "You've heard of it?"

"Lacey, it's only the richest borough in London. Millionaires live in Knightsbridge. Heck, billionaires live there! It's not for people like us."

That gave Lacey pause for thought. Being an outsider was something of a blessing in this case, because while she knew the company was well respected on the antiquing scene, it hadn't occurred to her quite how high-class it really was. If its auction house was located in the most expensive part of London, then presumably that meant they handled only the most expensive of items, for the richest of clientele. Being an auctioneer in a place like that would be a huge step on her career ladder. The thought of it made Lacey's ambitious side suddenly rev to life.

"I'm not suggesting we live *in* Knightsbridge," Lacey said. "Most people who work in London live on the outskirts, don't they, and take the Tube in?"

Tom pulled a face. "You would hate living in London. I promise you. Don't you remember why you left New York in the first place?"

Lacey bristled. Her leaving New York had had nothing to do with it being too busy or fast-paced, and everything to do with her ex-husband dumping her because he wanted a younger and more fertile baby maker. And Tom's whole attitude was riling her now. He was being dismissive. Even if she wasn't planning on taking the job offer, what was so bad about considering it?

"So that's that?" she said, suddenly testy. "Dismiss it right away?"

Tom looked perplexed at her change in tone. "You weren't actually considering it?"

"No," Lacey replied. Then she amended her answer. "Maybe." She sighed. "I don't know. It's not like we ever discussed our future. And opportunities like this don't come along very often."

She ought to know. It had taken her fourteen years to get an opportunity to change her life, and she hadn't looked back since.

"But we both have businesses," Tom reasoned. "Thriving businesses that we love. Why would you want to work for other people all over again?"

Lacey considered it. "Because I hold small auctions to audiences of a few dozen. If I worked for a big auction house, I'd be selling some really exciting things. Things worth millions of pounds to buyers from all over the world. I'd be handling famous items and selling them to famous people."

Tom pulled a face. "Since when did any of that stuff ever matter to you?"

He didn't say "shallow stuff," but it was implied in his tone. Lacey felt her defenses go up even more.

"You do know I used to attend auctions all over the world for Saskia when I worked at the interior design firm?" she said. "I went to Milan at least once a year. I've been all over Europe on business trips. You shouldn't be surprised to learn there's a part of me that actually likes the finer things in life."

Tom looked lost, as if Lacey had answered a question he wasn't aware he'd asked.

"Okay," he said cautiously. "But it doesn't beat living by the seaside and being your own boss. At least, that's what you always say."

Lacey pressed her lips together. He was right. She did always say that. But it was his decisiveness and rigidity that was annoying her, like the conversation was over before it had ever begun. He wasn't even willing to entertain the notion that they might one day wish to live elsewhere, or do other jobs. Lacey couldn't help but feel like he was unwilling to get to know the other side of her, the one that had existed before she'd left New York. The one, she realized now, she'd been doing everything in her power to stamp out of existence.

"I told them I'd think about it," she said with an air of finality. "They're sending me a package through the post, and I have a few weeks to make my decision."

"Cool," Tom said, distractedly. His focus had already gone back to his cooking.

Lacey sighed and let the discussion fade away. She'd sprung it on him out of nowhere, after all, just as the original job offer had been sprung on her out of nowhere. She shouldn't expect so much from him right off the bat.

Besides, it wasn't the craziest thing that had happened to her today. That title belonged to the strange empty envelope her father had sent her. If she exhausted Tom's reserves discussing the job offer, he'd have nothing left for that admittedly more important event.

Her stomach flipped as she realized she'd have to tell him she'd finally opened the letter.

CHAPTER SIX

Lacey put her cutlery down with a tinkle. She couldn't eat another bite. The meal of salmon and sauteed green beans with garlic had been amazing, and Tom's decadent bread pudding had been quite the treat. Brown sugar still lingered on her taste buds, mixing perfectly with the sharp tang of the fresh cranberries.

Lacey glanced at her handsome beau across the round wooden window table, framed by the beautiful ocean view out of the window. From his basket beside the back door, Chester snored loudly. Lacey was struck by just how lucky she truly was.

"Did I tell you Mom thinks we should have reindeer at the wedding?" she said.

From his seat opposite, Tom laughed. He was good-humored. He laughed easily. It was one of his best qualities, and one of the things Lacey loved the most about him.

"Oh dear," he said. "I'm not sure about that. Aren't they supposed to be a bit smelly?"

Lacey shrugged. "I've no idea. I told her the theme is Rustic Romance, and that we're hoping for more of a winter wonderland. She seems to have gotten Christmas grotto stuck in her head."

Tom laughed again. "Oh, Shirley," he said affectionately.

Tom's relationship with her mom was hugely comforting for Lacey. While mother and daughter could easily rub one another the wrong way, Tom always approached everything with an easygoing attitude. He was a natural peacekeeper, a mediator between the two of them. Just having him in her life had helped Lacey heal from some of the long-standing issues she had toward her mom.

Of course the same could not be said for her father. Tom had never met Frank. Lacey wondered now, after opening the letter and finding it empty, whether he ever actually would.

She clutched her wine glass tightly in both hands. It was time to rip off the Band-Aid. She'd discussed literally every single other topic she possibly could, right down to her mother's reindeer suggestion. There was no delaying it anymore. It was now or never.

"I opened my dad's letter today," she announced.

Tom's eyebrows went up to his hairline with astonishment. "You're full of bombshells today," he said.

"I know," Lacey replied.

Just like Gina, Tom had heard her repeated mantra that she'd open the letter tomorrow for the last few weeks. He'd probably just assumed she was never actually going to do it.

He reached across the table and lightly touched her arm with his hand. "What did he say?"

"That's the thing," Lacey said. "There wasn't a letter inside."

Tom frowned. "Was there a card?"

Lacey shook her head. "There was absolutely nothing. It was empty."

She shifted in her seat and retrieved the envelope from the back pocket of her jeans, as if needing the physical evidence to prove the absurdity of it.

She handed it across the table to him, chewing her lip with consternation as she watched him inspect it inside and out. He looked just as perplexed as Lacey had felt when she'd opened it and discovered it to be empty.

"Why would your dad send you an empty envelope?" he said, handing it back to her.

Lacey shrugged as she took the envelope. "I wondered the same thing." She stared at it, at the next jigsaw piece in the puzzle of her father's disappearance. "Do you think it's a clue?"

Tom fidgeted. His hand went back to her arm, only this time, he squeezed it gently. "If it is, I think it's his way of saying he doesn't want to be found."

He said it in a gentle voice, but Lacey pulled back suddenly, as if his words were a slap. After all the effort she'd put into tracing her father, having Tom suggest he was trying to tell her to back off was beyond hurtful. And it was not something she was willing to accept.

"No. There has to be more to it than that," she said, firmly. "Why send anything at all if he wants to be left alone? Why give Jonty Sawyer a forwarding address in the first place if he didn't want to be found?"

She could hear the childlike desperation in her own voice.

Tom looked at a complete loss. When it came to theories about Lacey's missing father's whereabouts, they'd drained the well months ago. He'd listened to her go over and over the same theories again and again, with nothing ever coming to anything.

"I don't know," he said, sounding exhausted. "Why give a forwarding address to an auctioneer of all people? Why close down his store in Canterbury and move to Rye, only to move on again? When has any decision your father's ever made, made any sense at all?"

He seemed frustrated. Exasperated, even. The emotional toll of Lacey's father's disappearance had worn him out after just a few months. But Lacey had been living with it for over twenty years. And she wasn't about to give up. Not now. Not when it felt like she'd gotten so close. Whether she had Tom's support or not, she was pressing on.

She stared down at the envelope, desperate to understand what it meant.

Then, suddenly, under the bright lights of Crag Cottage's kitchen, she noticed something she'd failed to before in the dim light of her store. Written very faintly, in pencil, on the back flap of the envelope, was a return address.

Lacey's heart flew into her mouth.

It wasn't over. Her father *had* given her another clue. Tom was wrong.

A surge of hope fluttered in her chest. She clutched the envelope tightly, feeling tears prick in her eyes. Her hopes of finding her long-lost father were still alive. She decided to keep that hope to herself for now.

Her mind began to race as she tried to make sense of it. What was her father trying to tell her? That he wanted to speak but he didn't feel comfortable doing so through the postal service? Or that he didn't want to be the one to start the conversation and wanted her to have the first word?

Lacey made a resolution to herself. Once her auction was over, she would make the first move. And she didn't want to leave anything to chance. No more waiting in the dark. She would go to the return address on the envelope. She would find her father.

With a fire lit inside of her, Lacey decided to throw herself into auction preparations, starting first thing next morning.

CHAPTER SEVEN

"What image do you want me to use on the website?" Finnbar asked, looking up from the laptop.

The shop had been a flurry of activity all day. It was all hands on deck to get everything ready in time for tomorrow's auction, especially since everyone wanted to attend the Halloween party at the Lodge this evening.

Lacey glanced over at her eclectic haul. She'd purchased some black crushed velvet to cover the display shelves in, and all her oddities were looking rather appealing if she did say so herself.

Her gaze was drawn to the rune-covered tome.

"The book," she said. "It's the creepiest thing here in my opinion."

Which was saying a lot, considering a real skeleton was part of the collection. But none of the other items gave Lacey chills in quite the same way the strange book did, nor made Chester growl.

Finnbar fetched the book and leafed through the pages.

"I'd agree with that," Finnbar said. "Any idea what its history is?"

Typical that the history student would be so curious, Lacey thought. But she was curious too. She needed to value it, after all.

"None," she said. "I don't even recognize the language."

"It looks obsolete," Finnbar told her. "Maybe a form of Latin, or Old French?" He flipped it over. "There isn't even an author's name on it."

"No date either," Lacey added.

"A real mystery," Finnbar said with a chuckle. He propped it up and took a photo on his phone.

"You can say that again," Lacey replied.

Just then, the shop bell tinkled. Lacey looked up, expecting to see Gina returning from the print shop with the posters. Despite the unfortunate mishap of last auction's posters, Lacey had still tasked Gina with the flyers and posters because she was much better at sweet talking the men into fast-tracking the work.

But it was not Gina. It was Taryn.

Lacey deflated. It was never good news when Taryn was present.

"Your decorations are horrible," Taryn declared, as she thundered inside.

Lacey glanced around at Gina's OTT decorations. They looked like they'd been purchased from the cheapest bargain bin party store she could find.

"I know," she replied with a sigh.

Taryn opened her mouth to say something more, then closed it again. She'd obviously come in expecting a fight and it had taken her by surprise when Lacey had agreed with her.

"What are they for anyway?" she continued, though some of the bluster had left her.

Lacey shrugged. "Beats me. I'm still not even sure exactly what we're supposed to be celebrating."

"In this town, dead witches, apparently," Taryn said, grimacing at a plastic spider dangling from the ceiling. "But how covering the windows in gaudy tat and eating too much candy achieves that, I'll never know."

Lacey nodded. She couldn't quite believe she was actually agreeing with Taryn on something. It had taken nearly a year, but at last the two women had found some common ground.

"Can I help you with anything?" Lacey asked. "Or did you just want to vent about the holiday?"

Taryn gave her a withering look but didn't answer the question. It seemed she had no witty retort since they actually agreed for once.

Finnbar looked up from his laptop.

"Hello, Taryn," he said, politely, as he leaned his skinny frame across the counter to plug his cell phone cable into the USB port.

"What are you dressed as?" Taryn asked, narrowing her dark eyes.

Lacey hadn't actually asked him that question herself. She'd been too preoccupied with auction preparations to pay much attention to his and Gina's silly outfits. Looking at him now, she guessed Napoleon Bonaparte.

"I'm Logan Flint," Finnbar said, as he lowered himself into the chair.

"Who?" Lacey asked.

Taryn rolled her eyes. "He's a Witchfinder General."

"Wilfordshire's most famous Witchfinder General," Finnbar added. "The very Witchfinder General who caught Violet Jourdemayne."

"Isn't that a bit risky?" Lacey said. "Violet Jourdemayne seems like a cult hero around these parts. Aren't you worried someone will, I don't know, want to take it out on you?"

Finnbar just shrugged. He clearly was not concerned. He looked back to Taryn. "What's your costume?"

Lacey laughed. Taryn was dressed in her usual LBD. Finnbar could be quite unobservant.

"Taryn's not in costume," she said.

But Taryn interjected with a frown. "What do you mean? This *is* my costume. I'm dressed as a person who hates Halloween."

Lacey burst out laughing. Taryn probably hadn't been intending to be funny, but Lacey was amused nonetheless.

Lacey leaned on her elbows across the counter to Taryn.

"Are you sure you don't want to go to the Halloween party at the Lodge tonight?" she asked.

She was feeling generous, since Taryn had managed to be in her company for a good few minutes now without infuriating her. And since there really hadn't been any reason for her to be here, Lacey wondered if perhaps she was a little lonely and too proud to admit it.

"I'd rather stick rusty nails in my eyes," Taryn replied, dryly, completely destroying that theory.

"Ooh," Finbarr said, piping up. "That's a good idea for a costume. I might steal that for next year."

Taryn shot him a narrow-eyed glare, then marched away.

And order is restored, Lacey thought with a chuckle.

"So, what do you think?" Finnbar asked, pointing to the laptop screen.

He'd loaded the photo of the book onto the special auction events page he'd created. Along with the photo of the book, he'd added some cartoon skulls which Lacey wasn't particularly thrilled by, but there wasn't really time to quibble over that now.

"It looks great," she replied.

The bell tinkled again, and in waddled Gina. She was dressed as a magpie, and the big furry costume was clearly a bit of an encumbrance.

"Got them!" she exclaimed, waving two large rolled up posters over her head.

"Great," Lacey said. "Let's see."

She wanted to double-check Gina's creation to make sure she hadn't accidentally done anything silly like the time she'd put a donkey instead of a horse on the equestrian auction posters.

Gina unfurled one of the glossy posters triumphantly and held it out with a grin on her face.

On proud display in the middle was the exact same photo of Alice the donkey that had found its way onto her equestrian posters ... only this time a witch's hat had been superimposed onto her head.

Lacey burst out laughing.

"How did you even manage that?" she exclaimed, shaking her head as she chuckled.

"The boys at the print store suggested it," Gina replied. "They're absolute whizzes with technology. I thought it was rather funny myself."

"It is," Lacey replied. "Who knew Alice would look so fetching in a witch's hat? We might have to make her our mascot for every auction. I can just picture her in a wide-brim straw hat for a summer-themed auction."

Gina rolled up the poster again. She'd also had a bunch of flyers printed up, ready to be distributed at the party.

"I think we're all done," Finnbar said, scanning the to-do list of auction prep. He put a big check mark on the last item on the page, which was the posters.

"Excellent," Lacey said.

She was starting to feel quite excited now. Fall was her favorite season, after all, and if she'd found a way to make the blip that was Halloween more palatable, then it was all the better.

"Not quite everything," Gina said.

Lacey looked at her with querying eyes. "Oh?"

"You," Gina said, pointing at her. "Where's your costume?"

Lacey was in her usual jeans and shirt combo; the costume she'd promised her employees she'd wear was folded at the bottom of her bag.

"Do I have to?" she asked.

"Yes!" Gina and Finnbar replied in unison.

"And hurry," Gina added. "The cab will be here soon."

"Fine," Lacey replied.

There was no point arguing.

She headed into the restroom and changed into a floor-length black gown. She added some dark eyeliner beneath her eyes and covered her lips in bright red lipstick, before smudging it with the back of her hand to give the impression of smeared blood.

"Ta-da!" she announced as she headed back to the main shop floor to see the others.

Gina let out an exclamation of delight. "Are you a vampire?"

"I guess," Lacey said. "Or a ghost." She shrugged. "Or just a goth."

"Well, whatever you are, it's perfect," Gina said. "There's just one thing missing."

"Oh?" Lacey replied.

Gina held up the alien antennas for Chester and raised her eyebrows at Lacey. "He's the only one not in costume..." she said, leadingly.

Lacey looked over at the two English Shepherds. Boudicca's devil horns had now been complemented with a shimmery red cape, which she seemed absolutely thrilled about.

Lacey sighed with defeat. "You can try if you must, but I don't think he'll let you."

"We'll see about that," Gina replied.

She approached Chester and attached his silly googly antennas. To Lacey's astonishment, he not only placidly allowed her to, but he looked about as pleased as Boudica to be wearing them.

"I take it back!" Lacey exclaimed.

She had to admit the two dogs did look adorable side by side like that.

"The taxi's here," Finnbar said from the door.

Lacey collected her purse and headed out to where the six-seater cab was idling beside the sidewalk. Tom—a robot—and his assistant Emmanuel—a zombie—were waiting inside for them.

Lacey quickly locked up the store, growing more excited by the second for the party.

But just as she headed to the cab to join them, a large stray black cat streaked across her path, nearly tripping her.

Gina caught her by the elbow.

"Oh no!" the older woman exclaimed. "A black cat crossing your path is bad luck!"

"Yeah, yeah," Lacey said skeptically.

She didn't believe in bad omens or any of that superstitious stuff, and it would take more than a black cat to convince her!

CHAPTER EIGHT

The Lodge was lit from the outside by a pathway of flaming torches. Creepy string music floated down the steps toward the group. With the first cold snap of fall in the air, and the smoky smell of bonfire, Lacey was finally starting to feel in the holiday spirit.

She flashed Tom a smile as they ascended the steps hand in hand. His robot costume was pretty impressive. He was wearing a silver jumpsuit, and had gone to the effort of covering his entire face in silver face paint. If it weren't for his striking green eyes, Lacey might not have recognized him.

They headed inside the foyer and Lacey let out a small gasp at the sight of it.

The foyer had been covered with beautiful draping black silk, and was lit only by candles in standing bronze candelabras. The water in the central stone fountain had been dyed black, and spooky doll's heads had been placed all around it.

Lacey shuddered and squeezed Tom's hand for comfort. "Looks like Suzy's gone all out."

He nodded, his gaze fixed on the dolls. "Very creepy."

Pretty twinkling fairy lights lit a path through the foyer and to the main door into the hallway, which had been covered in a thick red curtain with gold cord. A sign above read: *Enter if you dare.*

Lacey couldn't help but feel anxious about entering inside. If Suzy had gone to the lengths of pulling a bunch of dolls' heads off their bodies, then who knew what other kind of gruesome ghoulies she had lurking behind the curtains ready to pounce?

Gina clearly had no such qualms herself, because she hurried straight through, her stuffed magpie tail disappearing through the curtains. Finnbar shrugged and went up next. He was swiftly followed by Emmanuel.

Lacey and Tom were left alone.

"Lacey, before we head inside," Tom said, "I just want to apologize about what I said the other day about your father. It wasn't fair of me to judge him so harshly, when I have no idea what has driven his actions. I just hate the turmoil he puts you through, and it makes me protective."

Lacey smiled at him tenderly. "You don't have to apologize. You've been a trouper through this whole ordeal, honestly."

She paused, thinking of the faded return address she'd spotted on the envelope, the one she'd resolved to go and visit once her business with the auction was complete. She'd only decided not to tell Tom about it before because he'd seemed to be at the end of his patience. Now would be the perfect time to reveal what she was planning on doing. But instead, she held her tongue. Breaking such important news to her fiancé while he was covered in silver paint and dressed as a robot seemed inappropriate. Besides, she didn't want to give him any cause to worry. One night of fun with their loved ones was the least they both deserved.

"Shall we?" Lacey said, looking over at the thick velvet curtain.

"Ladies first," Tom said, clearly just as nervous as Lacey about what might be waiting on the other side.

Lacey smirked. "Actually, I think the etiquette is robots first, then ladies."

Tom chuckled. "How about we go at the same time?"

He held his hand up to her. Lacey took it, threading her fingers through his. Side by side, they passed through the curtain.

Once on the other side, Lacey immediately relaxed. There were no tarantulas dangling from the ceiling, no jack-in-the-boxes bouncing out at her. Instead, the hallway had been elegantly decorated. Far from the gaudiness Taryn had been prophesying about earlier, the party at the Lodge seemed like the classiest event in town.

Standing on the staircase were a string quartet, playing haunting tunes. Inside the dining room, a long banquet table was covered in buffet foods, with red candles in gold candelabras.

"Suzy has quite a flair for party planning," Tom said.

Lacey nodded. Her young friend had really outdone herself this time.

The couple found the rest of their group in the Drawing Room. Gina and Finnbar were busy attaching posters for the auction to the walls, while Emmanuel was standing by the bar waiting to be served. Lacey had already decided she wasn't going to drink tonight, because she had a busy day awaiting her tomorrow with the auction, but how she wished she didn't when she saw the inventively named cocktails available—from the Diabolical Daiquiri, to the Murderous Martini, and a Rum Punch in the Face.

"What can I get you folks?" Ash, the mustachioed mixologist, asked. He looked like he'd dressed for the occasion, but Lacey happened to know Ash always dressed that way, with a little handlebar moustache waxed into curls at the edges.

"Nothing for me," Lacey said.

Ash's eyes widened. "Are you…" he whispered, "…pregnant?"

"No!" Lacey exclaimed. "I just have an early start tomorrow. I'm holding an auction."

"Oh," Ash replied. "I can make any of these virgin if you'd like?"

"I'll just have a Coke," she replied.

"And I'll have a Bloody Mary, Bloody Mary, Bloody Mary," Tom said.

Just then, Gina came up behind him and punched him in the arm.

"Ow," Tom exclaimed, rubbing his arm. "What was that for?"

"You said Bloody Mary three times!" Gina scolded him.

"But it's only bad luck if you say it in a mirror," Tom contested with a pout.

The superstitious woman pointed over the bar. The whole back wall was a mirror, reflecting the bottles of spirits, optics, and Gina's own thunderous face back at them.

"Oh," Tom replied sheepishly.

Once they all had a drink in their hand, the group headed to the garden where the main party was happening.

The lawns had been beautifully decked out for the event. The wooden bandstand in the middle was draped in lace. Over to one side, a DJ in a big red hairy monster mask worked behind his booth. And right in the center, a huge bonfire burned. Lucia's oak tree effigy was waiting to one side, ready to be incinerated in the big red flames.

Lacey felt a thrill of excitement ripple up her. She glanced around at the partygoers. It seemed like everyone in Wilfordshire was in attendance, from Linda the hairdresser dressed as Catwoman, to DCI Beth Lewis, who was looking elegant as a corpse bride.

Just then, Lacey spotted Suzy, dressed in a floaty green dress like Tinker Bell. It was a very apt costume for her; Lacey often likened her friend to a fairy.

"I'm going to say hi to Suzy," she said in Tom's ear, raising her voice to be heard over the loud music.

Tom nodded.

Lacey began to weave her way through the tightly packed crowd, exchanging hellos with her acquaintances and complimenting their funny costumes on the way.

"You're here!" Suzy cried as Lacey popped out the other side of the tightly packed crowd. They were even closer to the speakers here, and Suzy had to yell to be heard over the music. She pulled Lacey in for a bone-crushing embrace.

"Wow, you're very strong for a fairy," Lacey said, laughing.

Suzy chuckled and spun around, showing off a pair of shimmering fairy wings attached to her back. She was a little unsteady on her feet as she spun back to face her, and Lacey guessed she'd had more than a couple of Diabolical Daiquiris that evening.

"What are you dressed as?" Suzy shout-asked.

"A vampire," Lacey yelled in reply. "I think."

"You look like one of them," Suzy cried, pointing to a group of strangers standing to one side of the celebrations.

Lacey looked over at the strange group. They seemed to be taking the Halloween celebrations very seriously, all dressed in extremely elaborate gothic attire. It reminded Lacey of Naomi's high school goth phase. As she remembered it, her sister had proclaimed she was a witch and started wearing pentagram necklaces and black lipstick. But like most of Naomi's phases, it only lasted five minutes before she'd moved on to something new—cheerleading.

"Who are they?" Lacey asked, turning back to Suzy.

"Guests," Suzy shouted. "Violet Jourdemayne fans. They're here for the effigy."

She jabbed her pointer finger in the direction of Lucia's incredible ten-foot oak tree, which was being maneuvered toward the bonfire as they spoke.

"They only called a few hours ago," she continued. "Talk about last-minute bookings!" She pulled Lacey closer and yelled into her ear. "Get this. They asked if they could bring their magpies with them!"

Lacey attempted to move her head away from her exuberantly tipsy friend, but Suzy was gripping her arm tightly with her pixie fingers.

"What did you tell them?" she asked.

"That we have a no pets policy!" Suzy exclaimed, giggling. Then she held up her index finger. "Unless, of course, they were guide magpies for the blind."

Lacey tipped her head back and laughed heartily. It was nice to let loose for once, to get some respite from the worries that had been plaguing her.

She eyed the odd bunch again and considered if perhaps they weren't in costume at all. Perhaps they were actual goths. If they genuinely had magpies as pets, they were probably pretty hardcore fans of Violet Jourdemayne. So hardcore they'd traveled to the place of her execution to watch an effigy of her burn.

Lacey didn't know a huge amount about the sub-culture, beyond her younger sister's flirtation with all things gloomy in freshman year. But she did know that they liked to go against the grain, not just with their fashion choices but often with their lifestyles.

The peculiar group were certainly curious.

Just then, Lacey spotted Lucia over by the effigy, waving an arm over her head at Suzy.

"That's my cue!" Suzy shouted. "Effigy time!"

She slipped away, disappearing into the crowds.

At the same time, the music changed to the "Monster Mash" and everyone around Lacey began to dance exuberantly. A flash of silver caught her eye, and Tom suddenly emerged from the wall of dancers.

His eyes sparkled with mischief at Lacey.

"Would you care to 'do the Mash' with me?" he asked, offering his hand.

"I'd be honored," Lacey replied, giggling as she slid her hand inside his.

Tom led her into the crowd, finding a small space for them to dance together. Lacey had to accept she was having fun. Being playful and silly didn't come naturally to her, and it was nice to let her hair down for a change.

She heard a *whomp* noise and turned in unison with the rest of the dancers to face the bonfire. The effigy had been maneuvered into it and flames began to lick up its sides, crawling up the fake oak wood and swallowing the ghostly image of Violet Jourdemayne.

The crowd cooed, but Lacey felt a shiver run up her spine. She tried to shake it off, but she couldn't.

That's when she noticed, from the other side of the bonfire, someone was watching her.

Orange flames distorted their image, making them waver like a mirage.

It was one of the goth men from the peculiar group of out-of-towners, Lacey realized. He was tall and willowy, with dark sinister eyes that didn't detract from the elegance of his black silky suit and ruffled shirt. Something about him seriously gave her the creeps.

And just like that, Lacey lost her desire to dance.

CHAPTER NINE

In her bed that night, Lacey tossed and turned, struggling to get to sleep. The wind had gotten up, and it ripped noisily through the crisp autumn leaves of the tree outside her window. Branches scratched against her window like knocking. The moon was full and bright against her curtains, casting shadows that looked like fingers tapping. It didn't help that Tom was snoring contentedly beside her, and Chester was snoring contentedly at her feet. She couldn't even take anything to help her sleep; she didn't want to be groggy for the auction tomorrow.

She stared at the ceiling, listening to the twigs tapping on her window. Then suddenly, she heard a distinct change in the noise on the French doors. It wasn't the scritching of twigs anymore, but a distinct *knock-knock-knock.*

Lacey sat bolt upright and looked toward the balcony. Her heart went into her throat as she realized someone was standing on the other side of the glass door, on the balcony, peering in through the curtains. A man.

Lacey tried to scream but no noise came out.

The figure knocked again on the window. Lacey realized she recognized him. It was the man from the party. The elegant man who'd been staring at her through the flames of the burning bonfire. Had he followed her home? Was he stalking her?

"Lacey?" a voice said.

Lacey squeaked with terror. But she realized the voice was Tom's. He was suddenly sitting up beside her, peering at her with concern, a comforting hand on her back.

Lacey gasped, her heart slamming against her ribs.

"I think you're having a nightmare," he said, gently

Disoriented, Lacey looked back to the window. There was no one there. Just the usual branches of the tree occasionally tapping against the glass in the wind.

Tom was right. She must've fallen asleep and dreamt the whole thing.

"Y—yes," she stammered. "You're right. It was just a nightmare."

She lay back against the soft pillows, settling into Tom's warm, comforting arms. He quickly began to snore.

But Lacey's heart was still pounding. The dream had shaken her to the core. She wasn't usually one for signs or premonitions, but she just couldn't shake the feeling that her dream had meant something, and that it was an ominous warning of things to come.

*

Lacey woke early for the auction. Despite having avoided booze at the party, she still had a groggy head. She'd slept poorly, thanks to the creepy goth man showing up in her nightmare.

She left Tom in bed to sleep off his hangover and headed out with Chester for the walk to work.

They headed down the cliff path and onto the beach. To Lacey's surprise, there were several groups of the strange gothic-looking out-of-towners, sitting in circles around smoldering bonfires. Considering it was a chilly autumn morning, the sight looked rather sinister.

Lacey shuddered. What were they all up to, on the beach at this time in the morning? Had they been here all night? By the smoldering bonfires, it certainly appeared as if they'd spent at least the last couple of hours down here. But why?

Lacey couldn't help but think they were performing rituals or something. She knew that was a prejudiced thought, but there was really no other explanation. The group had traveled here to watch an effigy of their heroine burn in a bonfire, after all. Now the bonfire had burned, what were they all still doing in Wilfordshire, if not continuing with their bizarre homage to their martyr? What other reason could they have for sticking around?

Lacey decided to pay it no more mind. She had plenty of other things to think about beyond some strange black-clad, witch-loving, out-of-towners—things like her decision to visit her father after the auction, something she'd not yet found the right moment to tell Tom about.

After the auction, she decided. *One thing at a time.*

She reached the bottom of the high street and stopped in at Wilfordshire's newest coffee shop. She had a long day ahead of her, as did her staff, and turning up with caffeine for everyone was the least she could do.

The Coffee Nook was quickly becoming Lacey's favorite coffee shop in town. It was run by a pair of polite Danish siblings—Jens and his heavily pregnant sister Freja. Jens had lived in Wilfordshire for a few years now, but Freja had only recently moved over with her family to join him.

Through the condensation-steamed window, Lacey spotted the sister on duty today. She was dressed as a Teletubby, her protruding pregnant bump making the perfect TV. She was busy serving a man who Lacey guessed was one of the out-of-towners, because he was wearing a black velvet suit and a long black cape that reached his toes.

"Morning!" Lacey said to Freja as she entered the store, the bell above tinkling.

She stepped to one side to keep out of the way. The store was very small. More of a kiosk than a shop, really.

From her place behind the counter, Freja flashed Lacey a tense hello. She looked a little stressed, and it didn't take long for Lacey to guess why. Her choice of costume had been very ill advised. She was struggling to key in the prices on the register, and fumbling in her attempts to make the coffee. The out-of-towner was impatiently drumming his long, black-painted nails on the countertop, putting even more pressure on Freja to hurry up. Lacey couldn't help but feel bad for her.

Just then, the door opened again, and the bell tinkled as Ivan Parry, the landlord Lacey had purchased Crag Cottage from, squeezed into the small store. He was dressed in his usual jeans and shirt combo, the only difference being the addition of a black baseball cap with plastic bat wings stuck on it.

"Morning Lacey," he said, sardining himself beside her. "I hear you're having an auction today."

"I am," Lacey replied, noticing the way his gaze went over her shoulder to the peculiar caped man, before a disdainful frown appeared on his forehead. Which was a bit rich, considering the ludicrous hat that he himself was wearing. "Are you coming?"

He shook his head. "Not this time around, I'm afraid. I don't think you're selling anything I'm in need of."

"What do you mean?" Lacey joked. "You can never have too much taxidermy."

Ivan chuckled at her joke.

49

Just then, the caped man turned from the counter, coffee in hand, and Lacey and Ivan squidged up closer to the wall to give him space to leave.

As the man inched past them, he took a sip from his cup. Then, suddenly, he spat it out everywhere.

Lacey turned away just in time not to get a face full of hot coffee spray, but she felt it splatter into her hair and grimaced.

"This has milk in it!" the man bellowed loudly. "I asked for soya!"

Freja looked mortified. "I am so sorry. Here, let me exchange it for you."

"Exchange it?" came his incredulous cry. "I can't trust you not to mess up my order again! If you weren't wearing such a stupid costume, perhaps you'd have heard me the first time!"

"Hey!" Lacey said, stepping forward. The man's outburst was outrageous, and Lacey wasn't going to just stand by while he shouted at a heavily pregnant woman. "You need to calm down."

"Calm down?" the man cried. "This imbecilic woman just tried to poison me with liquid from the mammary glands of a cow!"

"Okay, I think you're being a little bit OTT now," Lacey told him.

The man glared at her angrily. Then he threw his coffee cup on the floor. It hit the ground with a thud, spraying hot liquid into the air.

Lacey jumped back as the hot puddle of coffee spread across the tiled floor.

"I, Alaric Moon, curse thee!" he bellowed, glowering at Freja. He glared at Lacey. "I curse thee." Then he spread his arms wide and cried to the ceiling, "I curse all who enter these walls!"

With that, he swished his stupid cape around him and stormed away.

There was a moment of stunned silence. Then, all at once, the three inside the store burst out laughing.

"Well, that was ridiculous!" Lacey exclaimed.

"I wonder what curse will befall me?" Ivan added. He was laughing so hard, tears were plopping out the corners of his eyes.

"I'm pretty sure you were spared the curse," Lacey said, wryly. "Just me and Freja."

"And all who enter," Ivan corrected. "Don't *thee* forget."

Lacey laughed.

Freja came hurrying from behind the counter with a tea cloth to wipe up the mess.

"Let me," Lacey offered.

Freja gratefully handed over the tea cloth. "Thank you," she said, her hand going down to her stomach. "I don't think I'd be able to reach." She patted her belly. "I'm just about ready to pop."

Lacey bent down and began mopping up the coffee puddle.

"Is it normal to dress and act that way in England?" Freja asked, nervously.

"NO!" Lacey cried.

Ivan began to chuckle. "We all have Lacey to thank for those oddballs being in town!"

Lacey paused what she was doing. She looked up at him from the puddle and frowned.

"Me?" she asked. "What do you mean? They came here because of the bonfire, didn't they?"

"Right," Ivan replied. "But they're sticking around for the auction!"

Lacey gulped. She'd wanted this to be a good-natured Halloween auction for locals. She had no idea it would draw this sort of bizarre attention.

Ivan's chuckles died away and he wiped his tears from his eyes. "Poor Lacey," he said. "You'll be the one on the receiving end of that temper   tantrum   next."

CHAPTER TEN

With Ivan's warning ringing in her ear, Lacey hurried back to her store to warn the others.

She pushed the door so hard the bell almost came right off its hinges, and rushed inside with such haste she almost dropped the cardboard tray of teas and coffees.

"Gina! Finn!" she exclaimed.

Then she screeched to a halt. It was too late. Her employees were not alone. A tall, black-clad man was standing in her store.

Lacey gulped. The man was perusing the shelves, his long black hair hanging halfway down his back. Gina and Finn were standing behind the counter, staring at him openmouthed. They looked hypnotized. Perplexed. Confounded.

Lacey's first thought was that it was the awful Alaric Moon from the Coffee Nook. But then she realized the man had no cape on, and a little bit of tension left her body.

That was, until Lacey suddenly realized who it was standing in her store. Not Alaric Moon, but the elegant man from the party, the one who'd watched her through the flames of the bonfire. The one who'd made an appearance in her nightmare last night.

Prickles went up and down her spine. The man who'd spooked her to such an extent he infiltrated her nightmares was now standing in her store… and she would have to serve him!

Lacey quickly snapped out of her shock and switched on her professional mode.

"Gina, Finn," she said, shoving the takeout cups into the hands of her stupefied employees. "Please go and finish any last-minute preparations for the auction. I need to attend to this customer."

Her two employees took their drinks and scurried away, reminding Lacey of little children being shooed away from adult business.

She swallowed hard and approached the formidable man.

"Good morning," she said to his back. "May I help you?"

The man swirled on the spot. As their eyes met, Lacey felt the same uneasy feeling she'd had back at the bonfire. Only now, without a wall of fire to separate them, Lacey felt even more uncomfortable. And without the heat mirage or the orange glow, Lacey could now see his irises were so dark they were almost entirely black. His eyes looked like two black holes...

"You certainly can," the man said in a strong Northern accent. "But first let me introduce myself. My name is Eldritch Von Raven."

He held out a pale hand with long bony fingers.

"Eldritch...?" Lacey repeated.

"Von Raven. That's right."

"L—Lacey," she stammered in reply, as she took his hand and shook it.

"Yes, I know who you are," Eldritch said loftily. "You're the auctioneer. I wanted to speak to you at the party, but never got the chance."

So that's why he'd been staring at her through the flames? Because he knew she was an auctioneer and wanted to speak to her? He really ought to work on his facial expressions; Lacey could've been spared a fitful night tossing and turning in bed if only she'd known he had had no sinister intentions!

"What did you want to speak to me about?" she asked.

"I wanted to speak to you about one of the items due to be auctioned here today. I saw the picture on your website and wanted to get a better look."

"The book with runes on the front?" Lacey asked.

An arrogant smirk twitched on Eldritch's lips. "Yes," he drawled. "The *book*."

Lacey didn't quite know what to make of that.

"Of course you may," she said politely. "But please be gentle. It's very old."

With a disconcerted swirl in her stomach, she headed for the auction room to fetch it. As she entered through the arch, Gina and Finnbar looked over at her expectantly, like she was about to announce that the man in their store was the leader of a vampire race or something. She just shook her head at them, took the book from its stand, and headed out again.

She approached Eldritch. At the sight of the book in her hands, Eldritch's black eyes sparked. He smiled a pleased, but sinister smile.

"Here you go," Lacey said, handing it over.

Eldritch very carefully opened the leather-bound cover and sniffed deeply. "Delightful."

Then he snapped the cover shut, making Lacey jump.

"You have no idea what you have here, do you?" he fired at her.

Lacey shook her head. Eldritch had a very condescending tone, and an overbearing presence that made her throat feel dry.

"It is a very special grimoire," he explained. "Written in France in the fourteenth century and thought lost to time."

"Oh," Lacey said, surprised. "I thought it might be written in Latin."

Eldritch chuckled at her ignorance. "Old French, actually. Or the *langue d'oïl.*"

"And you said it's a grimoire?" she asked. "What is that?"

"It's what you lay people may know as a spell book," came Eldritch's haughty reply.

"A spell book? Like with curses and hexes in?" Lacey asked with a shudder.

No wonder Chester had shown such an immediate aversion to it. And while Lacey herself didn't believe in such things, she could tell by Eldritch's expression he was being deadly serious. He genuinely thought this was a spell book.

"This is the reason so many of my fellow occultists have come to Wilfordshire," Eldritch continued. "Our circles are small and news travels quickly. When the image appeared on your website, it sent quite a ripple through our community."

Lacey was surprised. She'd had no idea. Perhaps her fun little Halloween auction was going to be more lucrative than she'd realized.

"I would like to make a proposition," Eldritch announced. "I will buy the book from you now, before it goes to auction."

Lacey frowned. "I can't do that. It would be unethical. Especially if all these people traveled to town for it like you said."

"I will give you twenty thousand pounds," he stated. "Right here."

Lacey's mouth dropped open. "H—how much?"

When she'd been researching the value of old books, she'd been disappointed to see that most of them, despite surviving hundreds of years, sold in the region of a few hundred to one thousand pounds. Only rare ones fetched higher figures. For Eldritch to be offering so much, the grimoire must be very rare indeed.

"Twenty thousand," the gothic man repeated. "And I'll take it off your hands right now."

But before she had a chance to utter a word, she heard a commotion coming from the auction room—the feverish barking of Boudicca and Chester, the screech of a cat, a loud bang, and yelling.

"Excuse me," she said to Eldritch, hurrying away to see what was causing the commotion.

As she passed beneath the arch, she gasped in shock as a black cat unexpectedly came streaking past her legs, fast enough to almost trip her. In hot pursuit were the two English Shepherds, and before Lacey even had the chance to catch her breath from the first shock, they barged past her in a blur, almost knocking her over for the second time.

Lacey grabbed the wall to steady herself.

"Help!" came Finnbar's feeble voice.

Lacey looked up. There, on the floor, sprawled beneath the Victorian skeleton, was Finnbar. He was floundering helplessly, his arms and legs going like a dung beetle stuck on its back.

"Help me!" he pleaded. "Help me!"

Lacey sprang into action. She hurried to him and attempted to lever the heavy skeleton off. It had trapped him right between its rib cages, like the bars of a prison. The poor boy was already an anxious bag of nerves. This would surely traumatize him!

From the other room, Lacey heard the commotion of the dogs chasing the stray cat around the store, and prayed her precious pottery would survive the calamity.

"Gina!" Lacey called toward the open French doors. "Help me!"

She heard footsteps come running. But it wasn't Gina's feet that appeared beside her. Instead, she saw the black shiny boots of Eldritch Von Raven.

"About my offer?" the man said in his distinctive Northern accent.

Lacey glanced up at him, stunned. A boy was trapped beneath a skeleton and all he cared about was a book? He wasn't even trying to help!

"I'm a bit busy right now," she muttered.

Finally, she heaved the skeleton up and freed Finnbar. Her shocked employee sat up, pressing a hand to his chest. He was panting heavily.

Suddenly, the black cat came streaking back through the auction room and out the back door. The dogs went thundering after it, in a blur of barks and fur.

The whole thing had lasted barely a minute, and yet the destruction was everywhere.

"Well?" Eldritch pressed. He clearly had zero concern about anything but himself and his grimoire. His callous attitude helped Lacey make up her mind.

"I'm not selling the book to you," Lacey told him. "You'll have to bid on it during the auction like everyone else."

Eldritch narrowed his eyes. "Fine. But just so you know, the grimoire is cursed. It will bring harm to anyone who keeps it for too long or whose intentions for it are impure." He looked pointedly at Finnbar, as if he was the first victim to befall the curse.

"I'll bear that in mind," Lacey said between her teeth.

Eldritch turned and clomped away.

Just then, Gina walked in through the back doors.

"You'll never guess what I just saw," she said, jerking a thumb over her shoulder. "It was that black cat again!"

From their positions on the floor, Lacey and Finnbar glowered at her.

Looking perplexed, Gina took a moment to survey the strange sight. "What's going on here?" she asked.

"The skeleton attacked me," Finnbar said theatrically.

"That's a bit dramatic," Lacey said as she pushed herself to standing. "The dogs must've knocked it while they were chasing the cat."

She reached down for Finnbar's arm to help him up. But as he pushed up with his hand, he winced, pulling his hand in to cradle it.

"Ow," he yelped. "My wrist."

"Maybe I should drive you to the hospital?" Lacey suggested.

Finnbar shook his head. "You have the auction to do. I'll be fine."

He tried to push himself up again but this time yelped with pain.

"You're not fine," Lacey told him. "Come on. Let's go to the hospital."

"I can get a bus," he said.

"But what if it's broken?" Lacey insisted. "I can't let you get a bus with a broken wrist. Your well-being comes first. I'll postpone the auction."

"No," Finnbar said, suddenly firm and serious.

Lacey frowned, confused. Why was he being so difficult?

"You don't have a phobia of doctors, do you?" she asked. Knowing how nervy Finnbar could be, this seemed like the most likely explanation.

"It's not that," he said, looking up at her with his big hazel eyes. "You can't postpone the auction. You need to sell the book before anything else bad happens."

Gina bustled forward. "What is he talking about?"

"The book," Finnbar blurted. "It's a spell book. A grimoire. And it's cursed!"

"Cursed?" Gina squealed. She immediately started flapping her hands in panic.

Lacey let out a long sigh. Now that Gina had gotten a whiff of the curse, she'd never hear the end of it. Lacey herself, of course, did not believe the so-called cursed grimoire had anything to do with Finnbar's injury, although the reappearance of the black cat was a somewhat disconcerting coincidence.

"Guys, please calm down," she said. "I promise you the grimoire isn't cursed."

"You don't know that!" Gina exclaimed.

"Yes, it is!" Finnbar wailed. "And it attacked me!"

He cradled his wrist and looked at the grimoire with a terrified expression.

"The sooner we're clear of that thing, the better," he said, his voice shaking. "The auction must go on."

CHAPTER ELEVEN

After what Lacey had been told by Eldritch Von Raven, she was anticipating an odd bunch of people to attend her auction. But seeing them all come filing through the door en masse was still quite the sight to behold.

Broadly speaking, they were dressed gothically, but each attendee had their own unique style. Some were in black leather, with piercings and tattoos and big chunky boots. Others were in elegant black velvet dresses or skater punk attire. Still others seemed to be inspired by the past, and were dressed in shawls and veils. The thing they all had in common, though, was their interest in the grimoire.

Lacey watched them enter, gaze at the items on display, then home in on the rune-covered grimoire. It was causing quite a buzz. She decided that turning down Eldritch Von Raven's offer earlier had been a shrewd move; there were plenty of interested people to join in a bidding war.

Just then, Lacey spotted a familiar face entering the auction room. It was Alaric Moon, the cape-wearing, tantrum-throwing, coffee-spitting man from the Coffee Nook that morning. Ivan had hypothesized he'd be coming to her auction. Now, Lacey realized tensely, that prediction had come true.

Alaric glanced around the room. His gaze found Lacey at the podium and his expression registered recognition, followed swiftly by disgust.

Lacey squirmed uncomfortably under his mean glower. She could only hope he'd be on better behavior at the auction than he'd been in the coffee shop. She really wasn't in the mood to be publicly berated by an angry man in a cape.

Just then, Lacey was distracted from her ruminations by a very pretty young goth girl approaching her.

"Excuse me," the girl said through purple-painted lips, timidly tucking a purple streak behind her heavily pierced ear to join the rest of her choppy bobbed hair. "Are you the one running the ghost tour?"

Lacey remembered the posters displayed at the Lodge, the ones beside her own auction ads. The girl must've gotten confused.

"Oh, no, that's not me," Lacey said. "I just run the auction."

The girl looked embarrassed. "I don't suppose you know when the tour is, do you?"

"I don't," Lacey replied. "But my colleague might."

She looked around for Gina. Since she was a local and had been the one to actually hang the posters at the Lodge, she was more likely to know the particulars of the event.

She spotted her happily flirting away with a man who looked like he was from the Hells Angels. When their eyes met, Lacey beckoned her over.

"Yes?" Gina asked, as she joined them. Her cheeks were flushed pink from chatting with the man.

Lacey gestured to the girl. "This is…"

"Madeleine," the girl offered.

"Madeleine," Lacey continued, turning back to Gina. "She was asking about the ghost tour."

"I saw the poster at the Halloween party," Madeleine offered, her blush visible through her pale foundation. "I thought it was something to do with this."

"The ghost tour is tonight," Gina told her. "It's jolly good fun, and very spooky!" She looked at Lacey. "You remember the medieval ruins, don't you?"

Lacey's stomach dropped to her toes. Remember? How could she forget? The medieval ruins on the island had been the site of one of the most disturbing experiences of her life, when her attempts to solve the murder of an American tourist had almost gotten her murdered herself—by a woman she'd once thought of as a friend, no less. She hadn't set foot on the island ever since.

"I remember," she confirmed through clenched teeth.

"Well, that's where the tour takes place," Gina continued, in the same bright tone, oblivious to Lacey's discomfort. "There's a meeting spot on the beach where everyone congregates, then a short boat ride across to the island, then a historic tour of the ruins by lantern light. It's a highlight of the Wilfordshire calendar."

"It sounds amazing," Madeleine gushed.

"It really is great fun," Gina replied. She grinned mischievously at Lacey. "We should go once we've finished up here."

Lacey shuddered at the thought of returning to the island. She was about to decline, when one of Naomi's little pearls of wisdom popped into her head. Back when her sister was in her spiritual yoga phase, she'd said, *If you have bad memories of a place, go back and attach new, better memories to it.* Maybe this was the perfect opportunity to do that. To shed herself of the fear that had lingered in her ever since that horrible night.

"Okay," Lacey said, boldly. "Let's do it. Tom's been wanting to go back there for ages. And Chester would love to as well. Every time I walk him on the beach and the sandbar is out, he tries to run across."

She glanced over at her dog standing guard by the door. At the very least she could fight her fear for him.

Just then, she spotted the clock above the door. It was time to start the auction. A jolt of excitement and nervous anticipation went through her. She turned back to the others.

"I'd better go get into position," she said.

"See you tonight," the shy Madeleine said, motioning to leave.

"Aren't you sticking around for the auction?" Gina asked her.

Madeleine's timid gaze fell to the floor. "I don't know if I can afford any of the things you're selling. Everything looks expensive."

"Well, you never know," Gina told her. "That's the joy of an auction. You might just pick up a bargain. And even if you don't, there's plenty of theatrics to enjoy." She lowered her voice and pointed at the skeleton on the bronze pole. "I heard two of Mr. Skeleton's suitors are here. There's bound to be fireworks."

A coy smile spread across Madeleine's lips. She looked genuinely touched by Gina's attempts to get her to stay.

"All right then," she said in her quiet voice. "I'll stay."

"That's the spirit," Gina said with a big, friendly grin.

Madeleine took a spare seat in the front row, and Gina and Lacey headed over to Finnbar. Since his unfortunate mishap with "Mr. Skeleton," he'd iced his wrist and concluded it wasn't broken, though he remained utterly convinced he'd been the victim of the grimoire's curse. Lacey was glad to know she'd soon be parting ways with the silly rune-covered book, even if just for her superstitious employees' sakes.

Lacey took her position behind the podium and a hush fell over the audience.

And what a peculiar audience it was, she thought. She looked out over the sea of black hair, peppered with the grays and browns of her usual local antiques enthusiasts. The locals were by far the minority, and they all seemed rather intimidated by the eccentrically dressed goth folk surrounding them.

Lacey could not blame them. This wasn't quite what she'd envisioned either when she'd first decided to hold a Halloween-inspired auction.

"Good morning, ladies and gentle fiends," she announced. "And welcome to this special, spooky auction. We have some very interesting oddities for you today, so let's get straight into it. We will begin with this delightful stuffed squirrel dressed in a top hat and tails."

Finnbar brought the wood and oval globe case over from the crushed velvet display area, showing it off to the audience. Inside was the taxidermied red English squirrel, dressed up like the quintessential British gentleman, complete with walking cane.

"This is a genuine Victorian-era taxidermy," Lacey continued. "Back when dressing up stuffed animals was all the rage."

A ripple of laughter went around the room. Lacey smiled. She liked to warm up her audience as quickly as possible, and felt bolstered by their appreciation of her humor. Still, it was best to assume her spooky audience would need a bit more invigorating than her usual crowd, so she decided to start the bidding low and encourage the sort of theatrics Gina had mentioned earlier.

"Let's start the bidding at fifty pounds," Lacey announced.

Her prediction was right. While several paddles went up into the air, the majority of the crowd remained still. Her peculiar patrons were in need of some drama.

"Fifty pounds," she said, pointing at a punk man with a mohawk, before looking over at a woman holding up her paddle a couple of seats away from him.

"Fifty-five," the woman said, nodding her hair of long, glossy hair.

"Sixty," a fairly normal-looking man with gray hair and a black band T-shirt countered, raising his paddle into the air.

Lacey quickly pointed her gavel at him.

"Sixty," she confirmed, rapidly, knowing speed was the best way to get her audience riled up.

"Sixty-five," the glossy-haired woman quickly returned.

"Sixty-five," Lacey confirmed. "Can I get seventy?"

She looked over at the first bidder and he nodded, waving his paddle above his head in agreement.

"Seventy!" Lacey announced animatedly.

Her pulse leapt in conjunction. So much for getting the *crowd* riled, she was the one becoming effervescent herself—and she was only on the first item! She'd forgotten just how much she loved this aspect of her job.

"Seventy-five," the female bidder said.

"Eighty," the punk man replied, before Lacey even had a chance to accept the woman's bid.

A hushed ripple of excited exchanges went around the room, and Lacey felt her pulse quicken even more.

"Eighty-five," the female bidder said.

"Ninety," the punk man countered.

"Ninety-five."

"One hundred!"

Lacey's gavel was darting from left to right to left, pointing across the room between the male bidder and the female bidder as they clambered to win the bizarre taxidermied squirrel.

"One hundred and fifty!" the woman yelled, now on her feet, her paddle held high over her head.

Lacey, eyebrows raised in astonishment, heart pounding with adrenaline, pointed the gavel at her and confirmed, "One hundred and fifty pounds?"

"One hundred and fifty pounds," the woman said with a decisive nod.

The people beside her were looking up with amused smirks. They were clearly thoroughly entertained. Lacey couldn't have hoped for a better start to her auction than the theatrics this glossy-haired woman was providing.

She looked over to the punk man. "Can I get one hundred and fifty-five?"

The man twisted his lips, as if in contemplation. Then he crinkled his nose and shook his head. He was dropping out of the race.

But that didn't mean the bidding was over. There was now a sea of thoroughly entertained onlookers, many of whom seemed to be on the edges of their seat. Lacey opened the bidding back to them.

"Can I get one hundred and fifty-five pounds from anyone for this delightful English red squirrel?" she asked, scanning the audience, making sure to make direct eye contact with as many people as she could.

There were no more takers. The woman with the glossy black hair appeared to be hopping from foot to foot now with anticipation.

"Going once," Lacey said. "Going twice... SOLD!" She banged her gavel and pointed it at the triumphant woman. "For one hundred and fifty pounds to bidder number sixteen!"

She banged the gavel again with finality, and felt her excitement peak. If she felt that good after just one item, that certainly boded well for the rest of the event!

As Lacey quickly jotted down the outcome of the sale in her ledger, the audience murmured with excitement, and Finnbar hurriedly returned the squirrel to its display. Lacey's staff were well versed now on how to keep up the momentum. Gina immediately appeared beside Lacey with the next offering—the scorpions in resin.

Her auction was already off to a flying start, and now that she'd gauged the crowd, Lacey knew how much to push, and in which ways.

"Next up we have this genuine antique curiosity," Lacey announced. "Circa the Victorian era, and originally catalogued as part of a museum archive. Let's begin the bidding at fifteen pounds."

She'd paid twenty for all four of the insects in resin, and was hoping that by selling them on individually she'd get a bigger profit.

"Fifteen," a man in black announced, raising his red paddle into the air.

"Twenty," a woman in black challenged.

"Twenty-five," a third person in black—whose appearance was so androgynous Lacey couldn't tell whether they were a man or a woman—countered.

"Okay, we have twenty-five pounds," Lacey said in her rapid auctioneer's voice, pointing at the androgynous person with her gavel. "Can I get thirty?"

"Thirty," the man said.

"Forty!" the woman said, waggling her paddle board.

"Fifty!" the third person said.

"Fifty pounds," Lacey confirmed. "That's fifty pounds for these gorgeous museum exhibition scorpions in resin. Can I get fifty-five? Fifty-five? Fifty-five pounds from anybody for two perfectly preserved Victorian-era scorpions?"

The first two bidders lowered their paddles, leaving just the androgynous person left. Lacey scanned the audience, looking for anyone who might be tentatively considering putting in a bid, but finding no one, looked back to the androgynous individual.

"Sold for fifty pounds," she announced, banging the gavel. "To bidder number twenty-four."

Ten times more than I paid for it, she thought, excitedly jotting down the winner's number and price next to the item in her ledger.

Despite the lower profit point for the second item, Lacey's dopamine hit was stronger. She simply loved auctioneering. The thrill was unparalleled, and she was especially glad to have finally found a way to actually enjoy Halloween!

Her employees had their orchestrated dance down to a tee, and as Lacey looked back up from the ledger, Gina was already there, having fetched the next item on the agenda from the velvet display—the ram's skull.

Even though it was the lowest ticket item, Lacey felt especially excited to sell this one. It was the first item that had lured her into the Ducking Stool pawn shop in the first place. It wasn't an antique, and animal skulls weren't all that difficult to find—indeed, she'd come across several during her countryside strolls with the dogs through the sheep fields—but it was a particularly attractive one, with very neatly curled horns. It was the sort of item a student would want to draw for their art exam. Lacey had decided to place it early on in the running to create a lull in the tension, before ratcheting it all the way up and steaming toward the finale of the grimoire.

"Up next we have this gorgeous ram's skull," she announced. "I'd like to start the bidding at ten pounds."

From her place in the front seat, the purple-haired Madeleine suddenly sat up straighter. Her eyes sparked with evident excitement. Lacey recalled how she'd said she didn't think she'd be able to afford anything on sale today, and she looked genuinely thrilled to realize that perhaps she could.

The young girl tentatively raised her paddle.

"Ten pounds?" Lacey asked her, with an encouraging smile.

Madeleine nodded shyly. She was quite evidently too intimidated to speak aloud, so Lacey accepted her bid with a smile, before opening it up to the rest of the room.

"Can I get fifteen?" she announced.

"Fifteen," the Hells Angels man announced from the back of the hall, waving his red paddle in an arc above his head.

"Fifteen," Lacey confirmed, before looking back at Madeleine. "Twenty pounds?"

Madeleine dithered momentarily, then nodded her head eagerly.

"Twenty pounds," Lacey announced. "Can I get twenty-five pounds? Twenty-five pounds for this gorgeous ram's skull, anyone? I'm looking for twenty-five pounds."

She scanned the audience. The Hells Angels man had lowered his paddle, and there appeared to be no more takers. Twenty pounds was about right for the skull, Lacey decided—she would break even on it, and the sweet young Madeleine could get a win. She decided not to push it any harder.

"Sold for twenty pounds," she said, bringing down the gavel.

Madeleine grinned widely at her win. And Gina gave her a wink.

*

The rest of the auction's items sold far beyond Lacey's expectations, so she was especially optimistic when the time finally arrived to start the bidding on the grimoire.

"Now the item I know you're all been waiting for," Lacey said, gesturing with her arm over to Finnbar.

Her employee picked up the grimoire and approached the audience, displaying it to them.

"A medieval French grimoire," Lacey announced.

The atmosphere in the room turned electric. A hush fell over the entire audience, as every pair of eyes fixated on the medieval spell book. It seemed to Lacey that everyone had become suddenly very serious.

Lacey had been unable to price the book during her online research, so her only guide was the enormous offer Eldritch had made to her earlier that day. She hadn't gone into the auction thinking she would attempt to get such an audacious amount for the book, but considering how well the rest of the auction had gone so far, she felt suddenly bold.

She found her courage and swallowed deeply. "I'd like to start the bidding at twenty thousand pounds."

Stunned whispers rippled through the audience. In the front row, Madeleine's eyes widened with astonishment. The locals, too, began whispering with shock. Like Lacey herself, they had no idea about the significance of the grimoire. But the goth attendees did, and Lacey quickly discovered she'd made the right call. A dozen paddles went into the air.

Among them, unsurprisingly, was Eldritch Von Raven. More surprisingly, Lacey spotted Alaric Moon with his paddle in the air. Him putting in a twenty-thousand bid on a book made his temper tantrum over a two-dollar cup of coffee all the more ridiculous.

She intended to ignore him for as long as possible.

"Twenty thousand pounds," Lacey announced, pointing instead to the mohawk punk. "Can I get twenty-five?"

All twelve paddles remained in the air. Lacey accepted the bid from Gina's Hells Angels man. "Twenty-five thousand pounds, thank you. Can I get thirty thousand pounds?"

Still, no one dropped out, and so Lacey pointed to an older lady with stark white hair, accepting her bid with, "Thirty-five thousand pounds."

Lacey could hardly believe it. She felt adrenaline begin coursing through her. Never in her wildest imagination did she think she'd be accepting bids for thousands of pounds! Hundreds, maybe, but not *thousands*. The book she'd bought on a whim was clearly some kind of important relic amongst this niche group of people, just as Eldritch had told her.

She felt her palms growing clammy from the excitement of it all.

"Can I get forty thousand pounds?" she asked, her throat suddenly drying up.

Eldritch still had his paddle in the air, so she pointed at him and he nodded his acceptance of the offer. It was *double* the amount he'd offered her earlier in the day. Lacey was glad she'd stuck to her principles and declined him now.

"Forty thousand pounds, thank you," Lacey said. Her pulse was starting to pound in her ears. It was actually becoming difficult to stay focused. "Can I get forty-five thousand pounds?"

She could hardly believe the words were coming from her mouth.

A few paddles were lowered, and Lacey scanned the ones still up in the air. She found one in the hand of Alaric Moon.

Darn, she thought.

She'd been hoping to ignore him, since he'd been rude enough to "curse" her earlier. But on second thought, perhaps a sweeter revenge would be to profit off him handsomely...

"Forty-five," she said, nodding in acknowledgment. "Thank you."

Alaric's expression remained haughty and arrogant.

There were still five paddles in the air, so Lacey took a risk and pushed the increments up higher. "Can I get fifty?" she asked.

All but three paddles were lowered. It was down to Gina's Hells Angels man, Eldritch Von Raven, and Alaric Moon.

"Fifty, thank you," Lacey said, accepting the bid from the biker man. She looked to Alaric. "Can I get sixty thousand pounds?"

He nodded, with an arrogant look on his face.

She looked at Eldritch. "Seventy thousand?"

Eldritch looked like he'd sucked a lemon. He began to lower his paddle.

"Sixty-five?" Lacey asked quickly. She was riding an adrenaline high and wanted to see if she could up her profit just a little more.

Eldritch nodded and raised his paddle again, though he looked far from thrilled.

Lacey felt a burst of triumph inside of her. She looked at Alaric. "Seventy-five thousand?"

Without even hesitating, Alaric nodded with a smug smile.

Wow, he really has money to burn, Lacey thought, as she turned her attention back to Eldritch. Sensing he was on the verge of dropping out, Lacey played it cautiously.

"Seventy-six thousand?" she asked, upping the increment by just one thousand rather than the five or ten she'd previously been able to fetch.

Eldritch looked crestfallen. He shook his head of glossy black hair.

"Seventy-five thousand and five hundred?" Lacey amended, quickly.

But Eldritch didn't budge. His paddle holding hand flopped into his lap, and he lowered his eyes, breaking contact with Lacey.

"Four hundred?" Lacey asked rapidly, lowering it even further. "Three? Two?"

But despite her cutting the excess, Eldritch had clearly reached his point of no return. And boy did he look mad about it!

Lacey was loath to give Alaric what he wanted after witnessing his outrageous temper tantrum in the coffee shop earlier, so she opened it up to the room for one final push.

"Can I get seventy thousand and one hundred pounds?" she asked.

But no counter bids came in.

"Seventy thousand and fifty pounds?" she tried.

Still no takers.

"Seventy thousand and *ten pounds*?" she tried in one final last ditch attempt.

"Just bang the gavel!" Alaric shouted.

There was nothing for it. No one was willing to put in even an extra pound bid for the grimoire. "Going once. Going twice. SOLD!" Lacey cried, banging the gavel. "For seventy thousand pounds to bidder thirty-three." She pointed her gavel with finality at the extremely smug-looking Alaric Moon.

Everyone turned to look at him, whispering their astonishment at the enormous sum of money he was willing to part ways with.

Lacey was just as astonished at the rest of them. She felt light-headed with excitement. Talk about a profit! She'd sold an item she'd brought on a whim for twenty pounds for seventy thousand!

"Ladies and gentlem—men," Lacey said, so excited she stumbled over her words. "That's your lot! If you could please form an orderly queue in the main shop front and my two wonderful assistants will finalize your sales."

There was a hubbub around the room as people stood, satisfied with the result. The person who looked the happiest of all was Alaric Moon, the winner of the grimoire.

Riding the high of the final sale, Lacey watched the attendees begin to file from the room. Then she noticed someone going against the flow. A short, stocky man was attempting to shove his way inside the auction room.

"STOP EVERYTHING!" he screamed. "I demand you cease immediately! This auction is illegal!"

And just like that, Lacey's balloon burst.

CHAPTER TWELVE

A murmur of shock went around among the auction-goers still in the hall. All eyes turned to the intruder. The ones he'd rudely elbowed on his way in looked particularly miffed.

"I'm sorry, but what are you talking about?" Lacey asked, feeling very uncomfortable with how her auction had been derailed.

"I'm the owner of the store The Ducking Stool," the man said. "And that grimoire is not for sale."

Lacey gasped. She thought of the bored-looking goth girl on the counter who'd failed to find a price tag on the book and had tried to hand it over to Lacey for free. No wonder there was no price on it, if it wasn't for sale.

Lacey became very aware of all the eyes in the hall watching her and felt uncomfortable.

"Perhaps we could talk in my office?" she said.

The stocky man looked suspicious, but he accepted with a nod.

Quickly, Lacey led him from the auction hall and into the small back office, where all her wedding magazines and to-do lists were still stacked up around the place.

"I need you to give me the book back," the man said again. "It wasn't for sale."

"I understand," Lacey said, thinking of her low-ball offer the goth girl had accepted without a word. "But the problem is I've since sold it on."

The man's face flushed red. "No you haven't. I just saw it with my own eyes on display."

"That was an auction display," Lacey explained. "And the auction's just finished. The book has been sold. I'm not the owner of it anymore."

"You weren't the owner of it to begin with!" the man yelled. "It was never for sale."

It hadn't taken much to return him to his enraged state, and Lacey regretted having trapped herself inside a small space with him …

69

especially since his voice was clearly loud enough to carry down the corridor to the auction attendees anyway.

"I'm sorry, but I paid for the book fair and square," Lacey said. "Your clerk was going to give it to me for free because there was no price on it, but I insisted on paying."

"I'm going to kill that girl," the man said between his teeth. He looked at Lacey. "Look, I'll give you a refund if that's what it takes."

Lacey shook her head. "I'm sorry but that's not going to work. I exchanged money for the book and made a deal, and now a further deal has been made again, here in my store. All sales are final. Those are the rules. I can't go back on it, just like you can't go back on your sale to me."

"It wasn't *my* sale!" he refuted. "It was my stupid employee's sale, one which she'll soon find out has cost her her job."

Lacey frowned. As much as she'd disliked the grumpy girl who'd served her, she didn't want her to get fired over this.

"I hope you reconsider that," she said, in the same calm tone. "It would be unethical to fire your clerk over a misunderstanding. I asked for the book because it was behind the counter. If it wasn't for sale, that ought to have been made clearer."

"Ethics!" the man yelled. "Who are YOU to talk to ME about ETHICS? What is ethical about ripping me off, and profiting from my misfortune?"

His voice was getting louder and louder, and Lacey was more than acutely aware she still had a store full of patrons finalizing their sales from the auction. She really did not appreciate the man's accusations. Business wasn't personal, and she'd done nothing wrong.

"I will call the police if you continue this way," she warned.

"Good idea!" the man cried, grabbing the door handle of the office and flinging it open. "Call the police, and I can tell them about the theft you have so brazenly committed!" He directed his final words into the corridor, yelling loudly so as many people could hear as possible.

Lacey felt her cheeks burn.

She clenched her hands into fists. "They'll take my side on this matter, and you know it. You have no legal grounds to stand on. And if you want to buy the grimoire, you'll have to ask its new owner if they're willing to sell."

The pawnbroker looked furious.

Then, suddenly, his eyes widened as if he'd hit on an idea. He tore out of the office and went charging down the corridor toward the shop floor.

Lacey bolted after him, realizing she'd probably inadvertently given him the idea of looking for the grimoire and taking it back himself.

She raced into the busy shop.

Finnbar was behind the counter working the till. At the front of the queue stood Alaric Moon. Gina was holding his prized grimoire open in her hands, chuckling as she attempted to read aloud from its pages in the *langue d'oïl*.

"NO!" the pawnbroker cried. "STOP!"

Gina snapped her head up, surprised. Lacey rushed forward, panicked that the man was about to snatch the book from Gina's hands, and put herself in front of it. But the man didn't try to steal the book, at all. Instead, he appeared to have gone deathly pale.

He pointed a finger at Gina. "You read from the book. You're cursed!"

Lacey rolled her eyes. She didn't believe anything of the sort.

"Get out of my store," she said.

The man seemed suddenly eager to obey. He staggered for the door, looking terrified.

"Cursed!" he screamed as he ran. "Cursed!"

The bell jangled loudly as he hurried through the door and slammed it after him. Lacey watched as his short little legs pumped beneath him, carrying him along the cobblestone streets and out of sight.

The whole shop was completely silent. Lacey felt every pair of eyes on her. She was so embarrassed her cheeks became as hot as a bonfire.

Finnbar cleared his throat. "Let's get all these sales finalized, shall we? Don't want to keep our patrons waiting. I believe many of you have a ghost tour to get to this evening?"

Lacey snapped out of her stunned shock and nodded. "Yes, thank you, Finn. If you and Gina can sort that out, I think I'll attend to some office work…"

She turned and staggered away from all the eyes staring at her. No, she didn't believe the grimoire was cursed, just like she did not believe in Alaric Moon's Coffee Nook curse. But being yelled and screamed at right at the finale of her thrilling auction was extremely demoralizing, and she needed a bit of time to herself to get over it.

Suddenly, the ghost tour she'd been so reticent about earlier could not come soon enough.

*

"What a day," Gina said, turning the door sign to closed behind the last auction attendee to file out.

Lacey snapped the ledger shut. "You can say that again."

It had been quite a strange auction, and Lacey was more than ready to put it behind her. At least inducing a state of fear would take her mind off of the horrible experience with the Ippledean pawnbroker.

"Let's get to the beach," Gina said. "Finnbar, are you coming?"

"Not tonight," he replied, putting on his brown corduroy jacket and checkered scarf. "I have too much work to do."

They headed out of the store together, and Lacey locked up behind them.

"Thanks for all your hard work today," Lacey said as the shutters rattled down into place. "I hope your wrist feels better soon."

Finnbar tipped his imaginary cap and disappeared into the darkness.

The two women collected Tom from the patisserie and the group headed down to the beach. The dogs zipped back and forth across the sand, but other than that, there was no one else here. No sign of the ghost tour congregating. No sign of the attendants. The place was deserted.

"Oh," Gina said, looking sheepish. "I guess the tour must be tomorrow."

"Gina!" Lacey cried, shivering in her jacket. "You dragged us all the way out here for nothing."

"Not for nothing," Tom countered. "Look, it's a beautiful full moon. We can row over and explore just the three of us. It'll be even spookier."

He was being typically adventurous.

Lacey folded her arms. "And who exactly will guide us?"

"Me," Tom said. "I've explored those ruins a hundred times."

"And I'll make up the ghost stories as we go," Gina said with a chuckle.

"You two," Lacey said, giving in with an affectionate eye roll.

Tom fetched the rowboat. Humans and dogs alike clambered excitedly inside.

The moon looked beautiful reflected in the rippling water as Tom rowed them across the short distance to the island. The silhouetted ruins looked even more ominous under a full moon, with their jutting towers and crumbling, jagged walls.

Once they reached the other side, Tom tethered the boat to the jetty.

"Lead the way," Lacey said, climbing out of the little wooden boat.

They trudged across the distinctive gray sand toward the looming medieval ruins. The crumbling castle looked especially ominous tonight under the light of the full moon, and Lacey shuddered as memories from that awful night months ago threatened to return.

"Quick, someone tell me a ghost story," Lacey said, worried she was about to tip into a full-on panic.

"Which one would you like to hear first?" Tom said, in a spooky storyteller's voice. "If these ancient walls could talk, they'd tell you tales of death, war, murder, and revenge…"

Lacey hunkered down into her jacket, her stomach swirling ever more strongly. Maybe her coming here was a bad idea after all.

They drew closer to the jagged stone ruins jutting out from the sand, close enough to see the green moss and lichen growing in the crevices of the stones. Lacey's stomach twisted into knots.

"Perhaps we should head back…." she began to say.

But at the exact same moment, Chester's head darted up, nose to the air. He sniffed once, twice, his expression turning intense, then went charging off inside the ruins.

"Oh no! Chester!" Lacey cried as he was quickly swallowed up by the dark shadows inside. "Chester, come back!"

Her voice echoed through the abandoned corridors of the ancient building. Chester's distant bark told her he was going full pelt.

"He must've picked up the scent of an animal or something," Gina said, as Lacey peered anxiously into the ruins from the precipice. "I bet he thinks he's got some very important herding to attend to. You know what these English Shepherds are like."

She looked down at Boudica, who was lazily sitting by her feet paying no heed to anything going on. The older of the pair, she was often more mellow.

Just then, from the distance, Chester began barking shrilly. Boudica's ears perked right up, and she began to whine in response.

"That doesn't sound good," Lacey said.

She knew all the distinct tones of Chester's barks, and that one was telling her there was trouble.

Putting her own fear away, Lacey took off after him.

"Chester?" she called into the blackness, as she followed the sound of his shrill barks. "Chester?"

It was nearly pitch-black inside the ruins; even with the full moon above, the labyrinthine structure and high stone walls blocked most of it out. Lacey found herself plunged into a velvety blackness so deep it almost felt unreal.

Suddenly, she passed beneath some kind of awning that led her into what appeared to be a large courtyard between several buildings. With the open sky above her, at last there was more light to see by.

A very tall watchtower loomed before her. Beneath it, she spotted Chester pawing at something in the gloom at the bottom of the tower. He'd found something, something that looked like a large black lump.

"Chester!" she cried.

He let out a shrill bark.

Lacey hurried forward, realizing as she drew closer that the lump was in fact a body.

She skidded to a halt beside the still body and peered down. With a gasp, she realized she knew who she was looking at.

It was Alaric Moon.

CHAPTER THIRTEEN

Bile leapt into Lacey's throat. Her hands began to shake. She could tell from the unnatural position Alaric Moon was lying in that he was certainly dead. She stared, aghast, as Chester whined and pawed at the body in the sand.

In the distance, she could hear Tom's voice calling her. "Lacey? Lacey, where did you go?" but it seemed like his voice was traveling over thousands of miles to reach her rather than just the other side of the crumbling medieval tower.

Horrified by the dead man before her, Lacey tore her gaze away, peering up to the top of the tower from which he'd most certainly fallen. She squinted against the fine rainfall that immediately coated her lashes.

"What do you think, Chester?" she said, her voice quavering with distress. "Do you think he fell?"

Chester looked up from his frantic, futile attempts to revive the dead man, and barked twice.

Lacey looked back from the tower, forcing herself to look at the contorted body of Alaric Moon. There was quite a distance between the place he'd hit the ground and the base of the tower.

She gasped, a horrible panic making her heart skip.

"Oh no, you don't think he jumped?" she exclaimed.

Chester barked three times. His expression was growing ever more intense with every moment that passed without the dead man rousing.

A sudden thought struck Lacey. Chills went up her spine. She whispered, breathless with fear, "He was pushed…"

Just then, footsteps came thundering toward her. It was her trio of companions, Boudica the dog at the lead, with Tom close behind, and Gina bringing up the rear as she staggered after the both of them in her cumbersome, sand-caked Wellington boots.

Boudica reached Lacey first. Unperturbed, she ran straight up to the crumpled heap of Alaric Moon and began sniffing him in much the same way Chester had. Then the two dogs began conversing in their telepathic way.

Tom called to Lacey, "Is that a seal?"

Lacey turned to him and shook her head. She'd thought the same herself, at first. The curve of Alaric's black cape around his hunched form made him distinctly resemble the creatures that often congregated on the island, and Tom's brain, like her own, had obviously gone straight to the most logical explanation. But the reality was far more sinister.

"It's one of the out-of-towners," she replied as Tom drew to a halt beside her. "Alaric Moon. He was at my auction."

Tom's face immediately blanched. He looked queasy, and a grimace appeared on his lips. He grabbed Lacey's hand, and she didn't know if it was to comfort her, or because he himself was the one in need of comfort.

His hands were warm, Lacey noted, and a sudden thought hit her. She slipped out of Tom's hold and went over to Alaric, pressing a hand to his forehead. Stone cold. He was long dead.

The *thud-thud-thud* of Gina's heavy footfalls caused Lacey to turn.

"What the bloody hell is that?" the older woman cried, her gray eyes widening behind the thick lenses of her red-framed spectacles.

"It's a body," Tom murmured in response. He got his cell phone out and pressed his thumb down three times: 9-9-9.

Gina blanched. "A body? A *dead* one?"

Lacey stood and went over to her friend, resting a comforting hand on her shoulder. "I'm afraid so."

Poor Gina looked like she was about to faint. Or retch. Perhaps both. She reached a hand out for the tower to steady herself.

Lacey couldn't fault her for her visceral reaction. She, too, felt like she was suddenly in a dream. No, a nightmare.

"I'd like to report a death," Tom said into his cell phone, pacing away from them.

"Do you know who it is?" Gina asked Lacey, her voice quivering.

"It's Alaric Moon."

"From the auction?" Gina rapidly fired back in a panicky voice. "The man who bought the grimoire?"

"That's right," Lacey said, perplexed at her friend's sudden shift in tone. "Gina, do you know something?"

Gina had gone as pale as a ghost.

"The curse, Lacey!" she cried. "I unleashed the curse by accident, and now a man is dead."

Lacey had guessed three possible reasons for Alaric's untimely demise: accident, suicide, or homicide. She hadn't even considered the so-called curse.

She shook her head sympathetically. "The curse didn't kill him," she assured her friend.

"How can you be sure?" Gina shot back, panic making her voice squeak. "I read from the book aloud! The pawnbroker man said I'd cursed everyone!"

She looked like she was on the verge of breaking down. Lacey took her by the shoulders and gazed into her pained eyes.

"Gina, listen," she said, firmly. "There is no such thing as a curse. Don't torture yourself. Alaric's death is not your fault."

Gina's eyes darted left and right as she searched Lacey's eyes for reassurance.

"I promise you," Lacey reiterated. "This had nothing to do with a curse."

Tom stepped back to the group, returning his cell phone to his pocket. "The police are on their way."

Lacey nodded her acknowledgment, her mind swirling as she struggled to process what was happening. Just this morning, Alaric had been swishing his silly cape around the High Street, yelling about milk and cursing people. Now he'd been reduced to a dead heap.

*

The police arrived in their big, motorized dinghy, like a strange black monster advancing from the ocean onto the sand. Among the uniformed officers were the plain-clothed murder detectives, DCI Beth Lewis and Superintendent Turner.

"They sent the detectives," Lacey said to Tom.

He was still quite pale from shock. "What does that mean?"

"It means they suspect foul play," Lacey explained. "I know how Superintendent Turner operates. If he thought it was a suicide or a fall, he would've left the work to the officers already on the beat."

Tom gulped hard. Gina looked frightened.

"Murder…" she whispered under her breath.

Lacey left the word hanging in the air, and turned to watch the officers as they climbed from the dinghy and huddled together. Superintendent Turner was at least a foot taller than everyone else, and his long trench coat somehow gave him even more gravitas than the uniformed officers. The graying process of his hair was now fully complete, and in the moonlight, it almost looked like a halo glowing on his head.

Of course, Lacey knew better. Superintendent Turner might technically be one of the good guys, but his way of going about seeking justice left a lot to be desired. Not to mention his prejudice toward her as a foreigner. She was just glad she hadn't been the one to make the call; if she'd even suspected her name was being treated like a red flag, it would have infuriated her.

The group of officers dispersed, fanning out across the beach—one holding a roll of that dreaded, neon crime scene tape that Lacey had so come to loathe—and leaving the two detectives behind. They turned their heads in unison toward where Lacey, Tom, Gina, and the dogs were waiting on the sidelines.

"They're coming this way," Gina noted, nodding her head to them as they began their approach. She seemed terrified, and it looked to Lacey as if she was shrinking into her bright yellow rain mac, like a tortoise into its shell.

"We're witnesses," Lacey told her. "They're just going to take our statements. All you need to do is tell the truth. We've done nothing wrong."

Gina visibly trembled. "*You* haven't," she mumbled.

The moment Superintendent Turner spotted Chester, his expression soured. His gaze snapped up to the trio of witnesses, scanning them until he found Lacey. His eyes narrowed.

Lacey felt her hackles rise. She stuffed her hands into her pockets defensively, as Superintendent Turner closed the final distance between them with rapid, stomping strides.

"I should've expected you'd be here," he said, gruffly.

"How are you this evening, Karl?" Lacey replied, attempting to extinguish his combativeness with politeness. "Beth?" she added, as DCI Lewis reached his side.

DCI Lewis nodded her greeting.

In contrast, Superintendent Turner's snappily responded, "How do you think?"

His female partner shifted uncomfortably, as she always did when he was rude to the witnesses.

Superintendent Turner peered about him, his beady eyes like a hawk's. "Did any of you see what happened?"

Lacey, Tom, and Gina shook their heads in unison.

"Any noises?" the detective continued. "A body falling like that from a height like that would make one hell of a thud."

They all shook their heads again.

"He was cold to the touch when we found him," Lacey offered. "I think he was killed a while ago."

Superintendent Turner regarded her for a beat. "Who says he was killed?"

"No one," Lacey replied. "But you wouldn't be here otherwise."

The Superintendent narrowed his eyes, looking disgruntled by her astute observation.

"Do you think he jumped, Officer?" Gina interrupted, with a hopeful note in her voice.

"Not unless he took a flying leap," Superintendent Turner replied. "Which in my experience of suicides isn't how it happens. But then again, he was one of those goth types, wasn't he? They don't tend to do things by the book, so I wouldn't be surprised if they had a unique suicide method, too."

"Sarge," Beth Lewis said reproachfully.

Superintendent Turner ignored her. "Which one of you found him first?" he asked the group.

"It was Chester," Lacey said, petting her pooch on the head.

"The dog," he replied through clenched teeth. "I should have guessed."

Beth Lewis removed her hands from her pockets, producing a notebook and pen as she did, and poised herself to take notes. "Can you talk me through what happened, Lacey?"

"There's not a lot to tell," Lacey explained. "We arrived a short while ago, and Chester ran off immediately. I went after him, and this is what I found." She gestured to the dark heap lying beneath the tower, now surrounded by officers and cordoned-off behind tape that fluttered in the wind.

"And no one saw who pushed him?" Superintendent Turner asked, peering up to the top of the ruins. "Or saw anyone fleeing the scene? It's at least, what, fifty feet to the top? That's a lot of steps for a perp to run down in order to flee without a single person seeing anything."

"Like I said," Lacey replied, "he was long dead when we got here. Whoever pushed him was probably already off the island before we even got here."

Gina started to tremble. "Or maybe the reason we didn't hear anything is because it wasn't a person who pushed him at all. It was a spirit."

As much as Lacey loved Gina, she really wished she would keep her mouth shut right now. Superintendent Karl Turner was not the sort of man who had patience for, well, anything, and she suspected he had even less for all that mystical nonsense. And considering he already held a grudge against Lacey, the last thing she needed was Gina adding more fuel to the fire.

Superintendent Turner gave Gina a peculiar look. "There aren't meant to be any certainties in investigations, but I can say for certain that this wasn't the doing of a spirit." He patted her arm in a stilted manner.

Gina didn't look reassured at all. She began wringing her hands fretfully. She looked to be on the verge of blurting out something stupid.

Worried her friend was about to blame herself for Alaric's death in front of a murder detective, Lacey decided to step in and deflect attention.

"Could the perp still be on the island?" she asked Karl Turner. "Hiding in the ruins?"

"My officers are exploring every inch of this island," the superintendent replied. "If there's anyone hiding out here, we'll catch them." He looked back over to the dinghy. "That's all for now. I want you all to head home and await further questioning after the crime scene is secured. Beth?"

She looked up from her notebook. "Sarge?"

"Escort them back to the shore."

The female detective nodded. She returned her notebook to her pocket and addressed the group. "This way, please."

They headed for the dinghy.

As they went, Lacey heard Superintendent Turner's voice call out after her. "Oh, and Lacey?"

She paused and looked back at him. "Yes?"

"No trips out of Wilfordshire, okay?"

In that moment, Lacey realized her plan to visit her father was in ruins. In fact, her whole future was in ruins. Superintendent Turner had confirmed what she'd feared all along. He'd made her a suspect.

CHAPTER FOURTEEN

"Thanks for the lift, Tom," Gina said, as she wearily exited the van with Boudica.

Tom nodded. He looked exhausted from the events of the evening.

"Gina," Lacey said from the passenger seat, before her friend slipped away into the darkness. "This wasn't your fault. You do know that, don't you?"

Gina gave her a haunted look. She quite clearly believed she had unleashed a curse by reading from the grimoire, and that Alaric's death was her fault.

"See you tomorrow," she said, simply, shutting the car door behind her.

Tom reversed out of Gina's drive and drove the short distance along the single-track cliff path to Crag Cottage.

"Do you want me to stay?" he asked Lacey as she opened up the passenger side door.

Lacey knew he had an early start at the bakery the next morning. She shook her head. "I'll be all right. I've got Chester for company." She petted her dog's head.

"As long as you're sure," Tom replied.

"I'm sure," she said.

She kissed him swiftly, then exited the vehicle and staggered inside her cottage. The darkness and silence enveloped her like a welcome embrace.

She shut the door tight and rested her back against it, listening to the crunch of Tom's tires on the gravel as he drove away.

Chester nudged his nose into her palm.

"Quite the day eh, pup?" she said.

She headed into the kitchen and switched the lights on. As she sank into the round table at the window and dropped her head into her hands, her emotions caught up with her.

So much for her plan to visit her father. Even if she was in the right state of mind, Superintendent Turner had expressly forbidden her from leaving town. Instead of solving the long-lost mystery of her father's disappearance, Lacey had now been thrust headfirst, against her will, into the mystery of Alaric Moon's suspicious and untimely death.

She wondered how long it would take before her phone rang and she was summoned into the police station to give her statement and answer their questions. Six a.m., she suspected. Superintendent Turner always liked to get in early, to catch her in a groggy state.

"Let's go to bed," she told Chester.

He followed her as she exited the kitchen and trudged up the staircase, her legs heavy with fatigue. The moment she saw her bed, she wanted nothing more than to face plant into it, but she thought again about Superintendent Turner's penchant for early morning calls and decided to shower first so she wasn't caught out.

She headed into the bathroom, discarding her rain-dampened clothes on the floor. The bottoms of her jeans were coated in clumps of the island's distinctive gray sand, but Lacey was too tired to do anything about that now. It would be a task for another day.

As hot water cascaded onto her head, Lacey's mind turned to the Knightsbridge Auction House job offer, which seemed like it belonged in a different version of her life. She pictured herself in a crisp black suit, bringing her gavel down on a multimillion-pound bid for a famous statue. Right now, that seemed way better to Lacey than where she was now. She was always so embroiled in death and murder here in Wilfordshire, maybe she should just up and leave.

But knowing me, Lacey thought sadly, *the bad luck will follow me.*

*

Lacey was surprised when she was awoken by the shrill beeping of her alarm the next morning. She'd been expecting to be interrupted from her slumber by the loud knocks of the cops at her door, so it was a pleasant surprise to realize she'd slept straight through the night. And not even a single nightmare.

Wary, she got out of bed and peered through the curtain down to the lawn below. No sign of any police cruisers in the driveway or on the lane. No plainclothes cops mingling with the sheep. Maybe she'd been too hasty in assuming Superintendent Turner had made her a suspect.

She dressed for the day and went down to the kitchen to make her morning coffee. The whole while she drank it, she gazed out the kitchen window at the grisly morning, half expecting the bright headlights of a police car to cut through the foggy drizzle at any minute. But none came.

"What do you think, Chester?" she asked her pup, as she fetched his leash from the hook by the back door. "Calm before the storm?"

He barked in response.

She wrapped a raincoat around herself, then headed out into the brisk autumn morning.

Chester trotted alongside her as they made their way down the cliff path to the beach.

There really was nothing like a desolate wild beach on a chilly gray morning to amplify Lacey's melancholy state of mind. Even the ocean was gray, like a storm was brewing inside of it. Her usually relaxing beach walk felt like it was putting her more on edge.

The feelings intensified as Lacey caught sight of the island in the distance. Despite the moisture in the air, she could still make out the shadowy shape of the police dinghy attached to the jetty.

Had they spent the whole night out there, combing the ruins for clues? If they had, could that indicate they'd found an abundance of evidence, and were taking their time painstakingly collecting it? Did that explain why the cops hadn't shown up on her doorstep this morning, because they'd already found a piece of crucial evidence that exonerated her and solved the whole case?

For a brief moment, Lacey allowed herself to feel hopeful this whole investigation would be over quickly, that her worries had been ill-founded. But as she turned the corner onto the High Street, that glimmer of hope was swiftly dashed.

Clustered at the end of the high street was a sea of red and blue police lights. They flashed like disco balls, reflected back in the windows of the stores like mirrors at the fun house. And, Lacey noted, her chest sinking, they were all congregated outside *her* store.

She clenched her fists. So that's why the cops hadn't been on her doorstep that morning. They were waiting for her here, so they could make a huge public spectacle.

"Come on, Chester," she said through clenched teeth. "Let's get this over with."

She marched along the road, chin held high, eyes fixed dead ahead so she could ignore the stares and whispers of the locals as she passed.

The two detectives were standing in the road in the gap between their silver BMW and the police cruiser behind. Beth Lewis looked cold, hunkered up in a khaki trench coat as she sipped from a takeout coffee cup clutched between her beige knitted gloves. Lacey recognized the cup as one from the Coffee Nook, and wondered if the detectives had been in there earlier this morning asking Jens and Freja questions about Alaric Moon's milk-induced hissy fit the morning of his death. Or maybe they'd just needed caffeine.

Superintendent Turner had his backside perched against the hood of the BMW, his unbuttoned overcoat hanging open, his legs crossed at the ankles. He looked deceptively relaxed, but Lacey knew he would pounce the instant he saw her.

It was Beth who spotted her first. The two women made eye contact and Lacey couldn't help but think back to the Halloween party at the Lodge. Beth had been dressed in a corpse bride costume, and she'd danced around a bonfire to the "Monster Mash" just like the rest of them. That felt like a million years ago. Indeed, Lacey felt like Halloween Beth was an entirely different person from the detective standing in front of her now. Instead of a warm smile, all the female detective had for Lacey was a subtle mouth twitch, and it fell quickly back to neutral position, before she nudged her superior to alert him to Lacey's approach.

Superintendent Turner looked over at her, his eyes sparking, then pushed off from the car hood. He came strolling toward Lacey and flashed her his badge.

"Superintendent Turner," he announced, as if she didn't already know who he was.

It was all part of the public spectacle, Lacey assumed. A show for the benefit of the watching bystanders.

"Karl," Lacey replied, keeping her eyes fixed on him rather than the badge in his palm. She'd made a resolution to herself to address him only by his first name. Since he showed her no respect, she felt zero obligation to show him any in return.

An arrogant smile appeared on his face. He was only able to sustain it for a nanosecond. The facial muscles he needed to smile had probably atrophied many years ago.

From the fact he'd decided to publicly turn up at Lacey's store, and from the cocky demeanor exuding from him, Lacey guessed he'd come into possession of a piece of compelling evidence against her. She prepared herself for the worst.

"We had a couple more questions for you," Superintendent Turner said.

"You don't say," Lacey replied, crossing her arms. "Shall we speak inside my store, or do you want to do it out here with the whole world watching?"

"Here's fine with me," he replied.

Beth stepped toward them. "Let's go inside, Sarge," she countered. "It's cold."

Lacey knew she was actually intervening for her sake and flashed her an appreciative smile, though Beth did not return it.

Lacey took the keys from her pocket and operated the mechanism to raise the shutters. They rattled noisily as they coiled up on their rollers—pulling the attention of yet more curious passersby as they took their sweet time. Once they finally clunked into place, Lacey unlocked the door and invited the officers inside.

The tacky Halloween decorations had never looked more offensive to Lacey than they did now. She wanted to rip all the stupid grinning ghosts and ghoulie stickers off the walls and windows and stuff them in the trash. The sight of them served as a reminder as to why she was always so damn serious, never letting her guard down. Because anytime she let her hair down, some terrible thing came along and kicked her in the butt.

"Excuse the state of the place," Lacey said, turning to face the detectives.

"We understand the victim was known to you," Superintendent Turner began, wasting no time.

"I wouldn't say known exactly," Lacey replied. "He attended my auction."

Beth checked her notebook. "You also witnessed an altercation between him and Freja Johansson from the Coffee Nook earlier in the week. One where he supposedly 'cursed everyone inside.'" She read the last bit with uncertainty, her honey-colored eyebrows drawing together.

Lacey nodded. "Yup. That's correct. Freja got his order wrong and he started insulting her. I stood up for her and he threw the coffee on the ground and 'cursed' me."

She used air quotes to make it clear where her opinion stood on the matter, in case of any doubt. She was half tempted to add that if they thought her MO for murder was because she'd been "cursed," then they really needed to go back to the drawing board. But she held her tongue, because this was Superintendent Turner she was dealing with and he had quite the ability to twist her words.

"There was also another meeting," Beth continued, reading from her notebook. "During the Halloween party?"

Lacey cast her mind back to the Lodge. She didn't recall having seen Alaric there, but she'd been so preoccupied with Eldritch spooking her that that might account for it.

"I probably did," she said. "But I don't recall seeing him specifically. Alaric was part of the group staying at the Lodge, so it's likely he attended the bonfire with the others."

Superintendent Turner's lips twitched. Lacey suspected she'd inadvertently provided him with a piece of information he'd been hoping she would. She tensed in anticipation.

"Alaric's room at the Lodge was searched during the night," Superintendent Turner said, "as part of our investigation. We questioned the staff, the guests, everyone there."

Lacey could tell by how fresh-faced and clean shaven he was, that Karl himself had not personally taken part in the questioning. He had left that work for his subordinates to do, and was now here to reap the rewards.

"Okay..." Lacey said. She hated the way he tried to lead her. Whatever he wanted to say, he could just spit it out.

"He brought some very interesting possessions on his vacation," he continued. "I don't know about you, but tarot cards and Ouija boards aren't the first thing I put in my suitcase when I'm staying away from home for the weekend."

"You and me both, Karl," Lacey said calmly, while her internal voice screamed, *Just cut to the chase!*

"It wasn't all bones and pendants though," he continued. "Even goths clean their teeth and text their mothers." He smirked, clearly very pleased with his little witticism. "His cell was particularly interesting. There was a message on the screen, an unread one, from his local bank. You know the ones—*Unusual activity has been detected on your account. Please call us for security reasons.* Well, we did just that. We checked in with his bank." He paused for effect. "And do you know what we learned?"

Lacey took a deep breath. She knew where this was going. "That he'd just deposited a large sum of money into my business account?"

"That's right," Superintendent Turner replied. "He'd attempted to make a very, *very* large payment to you."

Lacey inhaled through her nostrils. "It was to my business, not me. Alaric won a very pricey item at my auction and we took payment on the day." She paused. "Wait. What do you mean he 'attempted' to make a payment?"

"It bounced," Superintendent Turner said with a hint of malevolent glee.

Lacey was stunned. She reached back for the armchair behind her, sinking into it. "The-the check bounced? Are you sure?"

"Yup," the detective replied with a look of triumph. "You didn't notice?"

"I didn't," she muttered. "No."

Gina had handled all the payments. She herself had been busy being yelled at by a deranged pawnbroker. Not noticing a seventy-thousand-pound payment get declined was quite the oversight. She wasn't sure how the cops were interpreting that, but even she had to admit it looked suspicious.

Seventy grand profit, gone, just like that...

"What did you say the payment was for?" Superintendent Turner asked.

"A book," Lacey said.

"Must've been a bloody good one," Karl replied.

Lacey gave him a look. "It was an antique. Medieval, actually. And very rare. It came from France and was one of a kind. It's technically called a grimoire."

Karl smirked. He obviously already knew all this, and was waiting to deliver his final blow. "Yes. A grim-waar. A spell book, right? Pretty easily identifiable, by the runes and yellow pages and black ink drawings of dissected frogs and all that. Funny that after we searched Alaric's room last night, we found nothing even closely resembling it."

Lacey's chest hitched with surprise. The grimoire was missing? Stolen or misplaced? Had the same person who'd killed Alaric taken the grimoire? Was that their motive for killing him in the first place?

As her mind raced through a million questions, she became acutely aware of the way Superintendent Turner was studying her. He was clearly watching intently for a reaction, so she tried her hardest not to give him one.

But it was patently clear to Lacey what was going on here. Superintendent Turner was off to a flying start building his incorrect narrative. As far as he saw it, Lacey had realized the huge payment from Alaric had failed and had gone to his room to steal back the book. At what point the detective supposed she'd turned the repatriation of

87

her property into a cold-blooded murder on a desolate island was anyone's guess.

"I suppose you have a search warrant," Lacey said, coolly. "Well, don't bother. I give you permission to search my store, because I have nothing to hide."

"How accommodating of you," Superintendent Turner said, with a sly smile. "But here's one anyway."

He shoved one of his yellow forms under her nose, then went to the door and whistled for his troops.

Lacey stepped aside as the cops marched in and fanned out through the store, ready to turn the place upside down in search of a grimoire Lacey knew they would not find.

As they stomped across the floorboards, Beth flashed Lacey an apologetic look.

"Sorry," she mouthed.

Lacey wrapped her arms tightly around her to keep out the chill that had blown inside with the cops. She'd have to sweep once they were done, because they'd traipsed dry leaves in with them.

"Sarge!" an officer called from the far side of the store. "Take a look at this."

He was holding something that looked suspiciously book shaped. Lacey's heart flew into her mouth. Had she been stitched up? Had Alaric's murderer somehow planted the book in her store to frame her?

Superintendent Turner thundered past her so eagerly, he whipped up the leaves into a tornado.

He took the object from the officer. From where she was standing, Lacey could see it was a thick, black, leather-bound book. Her stomach dropped.

"AHA!" Superintendent Turner cried.

He came marching back to Lacey.

"What have we found here?" he demanded, sounding triumphant.

Lacey looked at the book in his hands and was overcome with relief.

"I think you'll find that's the complete works of William Shakespeare," she said. "Are you a fan? My personal favorite is Hamlet."

Turner flipped open the cover and glowered when he saw she was right. He snapped the book shut with fury.

"This isn't over, Lacey," he said, menacingly. "I know you had something to do with this. And I won't rest until I find out what."

CHAPTER FIFTEEN

"You're scaring people away, Lacey," Finbarr said from the store door.

It was propped open to let in the breeze, since the day had warmed up considerably. Lacey, meanwhile, had spent the best part of the morning sitting in the creepy rocking chair in the window, watching the world go by as she mulled over the murder of Alaric Moon. She could see how the sight of a woman in a rocking chair staring off into the distance might spook potential customers somewhat, but she suspected the real reason no one was coming inside today had less to do with her and a whole lot more to do with the cops who had swarmed her store.

"It's not me," she told Finnbar. "It's that stupid stunt Superintendent Turner played this morning. Now everyone thinks I had something to do with Alaric's murder."

"Or," came Gina's voice from behind, as she carried over a rattling teapot and cups on a tray, "it's the effect of the curse." She placed the tray down and began pouring steaming tea into the cups. "Maybe the hex I read made the store invisible."

"It could've put a block on the door," Finnbar offered. "Like the ones that stop vampires from entering private residences."

Gina nodded her enthusiastic agreement of his suggestion. "See."

Lacey rolled her eyes. "If your hex had blocked the door, then how come about fifty police officers came streaming in through it this morning unimpeded?"

"I don't know, do I?" Gina said. "It's my first foray into the mystical."

"Did you invite them in?" Finnbar asked Lacey.

Lacey thought back to Superintendent Turner's search warrant. She'd distinctly told him he didn't need it because she gave him permission to come inside.

"Actually, yes I did," she admitted.

"Well, there you go," Gina said. She handed her a cup and saucer. "That must be it."

"I hope so," Finnbar said. "I'd prefer an empty store to more skeleton attacks."

Lacey shook herself. She was letting Gina and Finnbar get to her now. Her employees had been going on and on about the curse all morning, and it was starting to mess with what she knew to be the truth. She absolutely, resolutely, did not believe in any of that mystical, spiritual stuff. But Gina did, and she just wouldn't let it go. She seemed determined to beat herself over the head with it. Which was ironic, considering the actual thing she ought to be feeling bad about was the bounced payment for the grimoire she'd failed to notice. Lacey had wanted to challenge her over it, but didn't want to lay it on thick since she was already agonizing over the curse.

"You do know an empty store means no customers," Lacey told them both. "And no customers means no profits. Which means no jobs."

Gina gave Lacey her overbearing mother look. "You think we're talking nonsense. But you can't overlook the coincidences. The warning from the Ippledean pawnbroker. The black cat that crossed our path."

"The cat?" Lacey exclaimed, making her teacup and saucer rattle in her hands. "Come on, Gina! Do you know how many cats have crossed our path without anything bad ever happening?"

"Hey, look!" Finbarr said loudly, in an obvious attempt to interrupt their bickering. "The goths are still in town." He pointed to the street opposite, where a man and woman clad from head to toe in black strolled along the cobblestones hand in hand.

His diversion tactic worked. The women dropped the subject.

Gina joined Finnbar at the door with his cup of tea, and the three of them sipped quietly as they watched the creepy couple pause outside the patisserie and marvel at Tom's haunted gingerbread house, with a little ghost girl projected inside.

"Why are they still in town?" Lacey wondered aloud. "All the spooky festivities have finished now, haven't they?"

"It must be for the ghost tour," Gina replied. "I got the date wrong, didn't I? It's probably tonight or tomorrow or something."

"Surely it will be cancelled," Finbarr said, sipping from his flowery cup. "The ruins are a crime scene now."

Lacey shuddered as a memory formed in her mind's eye of the misty island and the crime scene tape fluttering in the breeze.

"Perhaps they didn't get the memo," Gina said.

"But one of their party was murdered," Finnbar continued. "You'd think they'd want to get out of Wilfordshire as soon as possible."

"If they'd already booked extra nights at the Lodge, they might not want to waste them," Gina suggested.

"Oh sure," Finnbar said in a sarcastic voice. "Better not waste those nights at the B&B their dead friend was robbed from…"

"Maybe Superintendent Turner asked them not to leave town," Lacey suggested. "Like he did me."

It was wishful thinking. Lacey suspected he'd only asked that of her, and that she was the only suspect on his radar right now.

Still, Finnbar had made a very astute point about the frame of mind of the out-of-towners. If they really were hanging about for the ghost tour, or to not waste their already booked and paid for hotel rooms, despite their friend's death, it indicated they had rather cold personalities. But cold enough to murder?

She watched contemplatively as the couple headed inside the butcher's.

"I bet they're stocking up on pig's blood for breakfast," Finbarr joked.

"Ew," Lacey replied, though she appreciated the light reprieve.

Just then, Gina's tone shifted.

"Uh-oh," she said. "Here comes trouble."

Lacey glanced over to see Taryn advancing along the cobblestones toward them. Her scowl was so deep it could probably be seen from space. Lacey braced herself.

Finbarr jumped back from the door to allow Taryn entrance. The woman gave him a sneer of disgust, before waltzing in and stamping her foot on the floorboards.

"I have a bone to pick with you," she announced, her dark, beady eyes fixed on Lacey.

"Really?" Lacey replied sarcastically. "I'd never have guessed. What's the problem?"

"The problem is all these horrible people you've lured to town with your stupid auction," Taryn huffed. "At least when you did the equestrian auction I could cater to the clientele, but these goths wouldn't know fashion if it smacked them in the face. I switched my whole stock to black for them, and they have the audacity to complain that everything's too neat! They only want to buy things that are ripped up or covered in moth balls. One of them even asked if I stocked anything that anyone had DIED in!" She threw her arm out at the goth couple as they exited the butcher's. "See! Look at that awful pair. It doesn't look like either of them have changed their clothes for a hundred years."

"I don't think you can blame me for the out-of-towners sticking around," Lacey replied. "The auction is over. They're here for the ghost tour."

Taryn shot her a look like she was the dumbest person in the world. "They're sticking around for that bloody book," she said.

Lacey frowned. "You mean the grimoire?"

The thought shocked her, but Taryn was certainly right. It explained all the nasty glances she was receiving. And it better explained the wide berth everyone was taking around her store more so than Superintendent Turner's early morning theatrics. Everyone blamed her for the peculiar out-of-towners infiltrating Wilfordshire.

"They're playing finders-keepers?" Lacey said aloud.

"Looks like it," Taryn replied. "Now they know how much it's worth, they're all trying to find it. The owner is dead, after all."

The revelation shook Lacey. *That's* why the out-of-towners were hanging around? Because they all wanted to be the one to find their dead friend's expensive book? It was even more callous than Finnbar's suggestion they were staying in their dead friend's hotel so as not to waste their non-refundable rooms.

Just then, a sudden thought struck Lacey. "What if they're not actually friends?"

All eyes turned to her. Everyone blinked, looking perplexed.

"What are you talking about?" Taryn asked with a scoff.

Lacey shook her head at her. "I'm not talking to you." She looked at Finnbar and Gina, and said it again. "Do we actually know whether the goths are friends?"

Finnbar's eyebrows drew together in confusion. "They all arrived together. They're all staying at the same hotel. They were together at the party."

"Sure," Lacey said. "But that doesn't necessarily mean they all knew one another beforehand. They very well may have met for the first time in Wilfordshire, at the party."

"And?" Gina asked.

Lacey wasn't sure yet if there was any significance to it. "I don't know. But perhaps there were some personality clashes. You can get some explosive situations when two troubled souls meet. There might be some motives in there."

"If it's a motive you're looking for," Taryn said, haughtily, "then you should start with that horrible Jeffrey Peters."

"Who?" Lacey asked, frowning.

"He's a pawnbroker," Taryn said. "From Ippledean. He came into my boutique after your auction with a face as red as a tomato. I was this close to calling the cops on him." She held her fingers up an inch apart.

"Why?" Lacey asked, stunned. "What did he do?"

"He stomped around the place like a caged gorilla, that's what, muttering about how he'd been robbed and how someone had to pay. I assumed he was yet another one of your disgruntled auction attendees. Honestly, Lacey, I think you need to work on your customer service skills."

Lacey jumped to her feet, standing so fast the rocking chair catapulted back and forth.

"Did that actually happen?" she demanded of Taryn.

Taryn grimaced. "Why would I lie?"

Lacey gave her a look. "Come on, Taryn. You and I both know your history of being silver-tongued."

Taryn sucked her cheeks in. "Touché." She crossed her arms. "Well, I'm not lying about this. That nasty little pawnbroker spent a good five minutes pacing my store cursing your name, and I can show you the CCTV footage if you don't believe me."

Lacey shook her head. She didn't need the proof. She'd heard enough. It was time to take action.

She stepped down from the raised window area, heading for the counter to fetch her car keys. Her heavy footfalls aroused Chester from his slumber.

"Come on, boy," she said.

"What are you going to do?" came Gina's nervous voice from the window where she'd left her.

"I'm going to solve the case," Lacey replied with determination.

"But how?" Finnbar asked.

"By heading to Ippledean," Lacey said. "There's a certain pawnbroker I'd like to have a few words with…"

Taryn's story had put the pawnbroker right at the top of her suspect list. He'd already shown himself to be a rude, mean person by shouting at Lacey in her own store. And by the sounds of things, it had taken him a significant amount of time to cool down again. Those were classic traits of someone with an anger issue, of someone so easily enraged they could snap and turn murderous at the smallest of provocations. And the loss of his grimoire was hardly a small provocation. Seventy thousand pounds was a lot of money to lose out on, especially for a small-town pawnbroker.

Feeling a fire light under her, Lacey snatched up her keys and headed for the exit.

But before she could leave, Gina held up her hand into a stop gesture. Lacey halted, frowning with confusion at her friend.

"What is it?" she asked, impatiently. "I've got a murder to solve."

"You've already forgotten," Gina said. "You're not allowed to leave town."

Lacey felt herself deflate. Taryn flashed her a triumphant smirk. So much for her and Taryn finally finding some common ground. The woman seemed to be reveling in seeing her suffer.

But Lacey was determined not to be beaten. She looked from one face to the next with finality.

"Then I'll just have to lure him here instead," she said.

And she knew just the way to do it.

CHAPTER SIXTEEN

Lacey headed into her back office for some privacy. As a general rule, she didn't like to be deceptive during her sleuthing, but considering how rude the pawnbroker had been to her, she didn't feel too guilty about it this time.

She picked up the telephone and dialed the Ducking Stool in Ippledean. She listened to the dial tone, until the call connected.

"Hello, Ducking Stool, Jeff speaking," came the distinctive voice of the pawnbroker on the other end. "Can I help you?"

Sure he's all pleasant now, Lacey thought, as she pictured the stocky little man standing in his oddly stocked pawnshop. *But just wait for the switch when he hears what I have to say.*

"Hi, this is Lacey, the auctioneer from Wilfordshire. We met the other day."

She chose her word cautiously. What she really wanted to say was "you yelled in my face the other day" but she didn't want to poke the bear. At least not yet, anyway.

Jeff's tone shifted immediately. He dropped the politeness and became suddenly cold. "Oh? What is this regarding?"

"It's about the grimoire," Lacey said.

"What about it?" he replied, a note of intrigue in his voice.

"I... I've had a change of heart," Lacey told him. "After our discussion, I decided that I should return it to you after all."

"Really?" the man replied. He sounded suspicious, which was fair enough, considering Lacey was actually trying to trick him. "And this change of heart has nothing to do with the curse your clerk unleashed? You're not trying to palm off any evil spirits back to me?"

"Not at all," Lacey replied, rolling her eyes. "I just decided that we small business owners need to support one another. So I cancelled the sale after the auction."

"Really?" he interrupted. "You're turning down a seventy-thousand-pound profit?"

"I don't mean to brag," Lacey said, "but I'm not exactly desperate for the money."

It was another lie. The money from Alaric had bounced, and with the case putting customers off from shopping at her store, it wouldn't take long for her reserves to dwindle, what with two salaries to pay.

"Are you implying I'm desperate?" Jeff replied with a scoff.

"Not at all," Lacey said, almost amazed at his ability to find an insult within her statement. "All I'm saying is the book is yours."

"How big of you," Jeff the pawnbroker replied, thinly. "Generously returning something to me that was never yours in the first place."

Lacey bristled at his sarcasm. He really was an unpleasant man. She was half tempted to tell him to stuff it and slam down the phone, but she reminded herself of the true reason for her call, and took a calming breath. She wasn't calling to quibble over old ground.

"You can come and pick it up any time that suits you," she said.

"You expect *me* to come to *you*?" came Jeff's incredulous reply.

Lacey didn't want to admit the cops had forbidden her from leaving town. If Jeff got a whiff of this being about a murder, her plan would fall apart.

"My car broke down," she said, quickly, thinking on her feet. "It's in the repair shop."

"How convenient," Jeff snapped. "First you steal my possession, then you make me go out of my way to get it back."

His comment chafed her. He sounded pissed, but better pissed than suspicious, Lacey thought.

"Look, do you want the book or not?" she pressed. "I can just as easily sell it if you're going to be so ungrateful…"

"If it's the only way to get the book back," he interrupted, speaking rapidly, "then I suppose I've no other choice."

"Good," Lacey said between her teeth. "I'll see you soon."

Jeff ended the call with a grunt. Lacey returned the phone to the receiver, rattled somewhat by the fraught conversation. Jeff was a difficult man indeed. Possibly even a murderer. And she'd just invited him to her store.

*

Not ten minutes had passed before Lacey heard a knock on her office door. Finnbar poked his head around.

"There's someone here to see you," he said. "Jeff Peters?"

"That was quick," Lacey replied.

Her lure had worked better than she'd expected. He must've driven straight here after their call. Jeff the pawnbroker was clearly very eager to get his book back. Or at least very eager to give off the impression that he was.

"Send him in," Lacey said.

Finnbar nodded and disappeared, leaving the door ajar. A moment later, Jeff entered through it.

Lacey was surprised to see him hobbling in on crutches, with a big black cast strapped around his foot.

"What happened?" she asked, jumping up to offer him her seat.

Jeff sank into it with a strained sigh and rested his crutches against the desk.

"I tripped," he said. "On my way back from your auction, in fact. The cobbles are rather uneven around my store, if you recall, and this blasted black cat ran in front of me. I tripped on the curb and broke my foot."

Lacey was glad Gina wasn't here to overhear that a black cat had been to blame for his injury. She'd never let it go. But Lacey, on the other hand, didn't buy his story for one second. It was too much of a coincidence that he'd get hurt on the same night Alaric was murdered. It seemed far more likely to her that he'd been injured whilst tussling with Alaric atop a medieval stone tower.

"What bad luck," she said, leadingly.

"Indeed," he replied, thinly.

The atmosphere in the room became very tense. Jeff was quite evidently suspicious of Lacey, and she of him.

"Anyway, enough of that," he said. He held out his hand, palm up. "The grimoire, please."

Lacey braced herself. It was time to poke the bear.

"I don't have it," she said.

Jeff's face immediately flushed red as his quick temper flared.

"What?" he snapped. "Where is it?"

"It's been stolen."

Jeff was so furious his neck and ears turned red. He looked like a hot tomato in a roasting pan about to burst its skin.

"You dragged me all the way here?" he cried. "Me! A poor injured man. And for what? A prank? What is this? What is going on here?"

He grabbed his crutches and Lacey hopped as far away from them as she could, worried he was about to whack her with one.

She held her hands into a truce position and spoke rapidly. "The man who bought the book at the auction is dead. In suspicious circumstances. When the police searched his possessions, the grimoire was gone."

Jeff looked stunned. Lacey studied his expression, searching for any indication that he already knew what she'd revealed to him. If he was the thief and killer, none of this should come as a surprise, after all. But so far, so convincing.

Jeff flopped back against the chair like a deflated balloon.

"It's the curse," he murmured, staring hypnotically into the distance at nothing before his gaze snapped to Lacey and turned into an angry glower. "I told you! Didn't I tell you? You had no place meddling with things you know nothing about, and now look what's happened! Some sort of evil force has been unleashed. The curse has struck! A man is dead because of you!"

"With respect," Lacey said, "I don't think it was the curse that got him. I think it was someone who wanted the grimoire. Someone from my auction. Someone who knew its true worth."

The pawnbroker's eyes narrowed.

"Oh, I see what's going on," he said. "You think it was me, don't you?"

Lacey shook her head. "I never said that."

"But you implied it," Jeff shot back. "Why else am I here? You don't even believe in the curse, so I can safely assume you didn't lure me out here for advice."

Despite his antagonistic and condescending personality, Lacey managed to keep her cool and remember what she was really attempting to achieve with this interrogation: to get a confession.

"How did you hurt your foot?"

Jeff frowned. "I already told you. I tripped on the curb."

"A bit odd, don't you think?" Lacey said, folding her arms. "You've owned that store for how many years?"

"Twenty."

"Twenty years." She whistled. "And in all that time you've never tripped on the cobbles before? Why so suddenly clumsy now?"

Jeff's eyes darted left and right. He was clearly getting hot under the collar. "I wasn't thinking. I was still in a bad mood after you stole my book."

Lacey turned the pressure gauge up. "Ah, yes. Your bad mood. You were in quite a state when you left my store."

"So?" he snapped.

"Took you quite a while to calm down, by the sounds of things, if you were still mad by the time you got back to Ippledean. Especially since you spent five minutes furiously pacing my neighbor's store."

Jeff squirmed in his seat under her interrogation. "And? What are you implying?"

"I'm implying that you were just as furious when you got back home as you were when you left the store. I'm implying that you're quick to fury at the best of times, and that losing out on a seventy-thousand-pound profit provoked a rage in you like none you'd experienced before. One that erupted into violence."

"FINE!" Jeff barked. "All right! You've got me!"

Lacey blinked, stunned. Was Jeff confessing to killing Alaric Moon?

"I didn't break my foot tripping on the curb," he said, his words coming out in one long exhale. "I lied."

"Go on," Lacey prompted. "How did you do it?"

"I… I kicked a wall."

Lacey stared at him with surprise. "You what?"

"I kicked a wall," Jeff said more loudly, this time through his teeth. He looked ashamed of himself. Embarrassed to be admitting such a thing to Lacey. "I have issues, okay? Ever since I was a boy. I was bullied mercilessly at school, and when I got upset, I'd lash out and end up doing stupid, harmful things. But I only ever hurt myself. I didn't kill anyone. I can prove it."

He reached into his pocket and pulled out a cell phone.

Lacey frowned with curiosity as she watched him scroll through his picture reel. What kind of evidence might be on his phone that proved he hadn't killed Alaric Moon?

He turned the screen to face her. "There. Feast your eyes on this."

Lacey took the phone from him and peered at the screen. She was looking at a photograph of an X-ray. It quite clearly showed a broken ankle. The name beneath it read Jeffrey Peters. The date and time matched those of Alaric's murder.

A wave of guilt washed over Lacey. She was wrong. Jeff wasn't the killer. He was just a troubled man with an anger problem.

"I'm—I'm sorry," she stammered, handing the phone back to him. "I got this all wrong."

Jeff put the phone in his pocket, his posture now dejected. He looked meek. Ashamed, even.

"I'm sorry, too," he said. "For directing that anger at you. But you can understand why I was so mad, can't you? Seventy thousand pounds! For a book my stupid clerk sold to you for twenty." He shook his head, looking desolate. "That amount of money would've changed my life."

Lacey couldn't help but feel sorry for him.

"If it's any consolation," she said, "the payment bounced. I never actually received a penny for the grimoire."

Jeff raised his downcast eyes. A small smile twitched on his lips. "That does help actually. A little bit."

He started to chuckle. Then his chuckles turned into a full-blown belly laugh, and his shoulders shook as he was overcome with joy at Lacey's misfortune.

"Ah, schadenfreude," he said, as tears ran from the corners of his eyes. "Is there any feeling sweeter?"

"I'm glad to have helped," Lacey said, wryly.

At least one of them had something to smile about. Because with Jeff crossed off her suspect list, Lacey was back to square one. It was time to break the news to her employees.

CHAPTER SEVENTEEN

"So?" Gina asked, the moment Lacey emerged from her office after her meeting with Jeff. "What happened?"

"It was a dead end," Lacey told her.

"But why was he on crutches?" the older woman pressed.

"It's a long story," Lacey explained. "A pretty sad one, really. But the abridged version is that Jeff had nothing to do with Alaric's death."

Finnbar joined Gina and the two employees followed her across the store in much the same way the dogs did when they wanted more kibble.

"So he had an alibi?" Finnbar asked. "An irrefutable one?"

"It was irrefutable, all right," Lacey said. "Pretty much signed, dated, and stamped. Trust me, Jeff's not our guy."

Her employees seemed to deflate. Like Lacey, they'd had high hopes that the case would solve itself quickly so things could go back to normal.

"But he seemed like such a good fit," Finnbar complained, looking just as disappointed as Lacey felt.

"He did," Gina agreed. "Although I can think of a better fit..." She paused for effect. "The curse."

This. Again. Lacey had just about reached the end of her patience when it came to Gina's belief in the curse. She added Gina's state of mind to the long laundry list of motivations for solving the case currently swirling in her mind and weighing her down, along with clearing her name, saving her business, not having to fire her employees, getting back what was rightfully hers, and freeing herself up to finally go see her father. Her poor friend wouldn't sleep easy until she knew an actual human being was responsible for Alaric's murder, rather than some murderous evil ghost she'd unwittingly summoned.

"We need to think about other suspects," Lacey said, grabbing her notepad and pen. "Before Taryn distracted me with Jeff, we were thinking about the goth group."

She wrote *GOTHS* at the top of the page.

"What about the guy who came around before the auction asking questions?" Finnbar suggested.

"Eldritch Von Raven," Lacey told him. She wrote his name down at the top of the list, picturing the willowy man in his black silk suit. "That's a good idea. He obviously wanted the grimoire, since he tried to buy it outright before the auction. And he was bidding on it for ages until the price was pushed up beyond his means and he dropped out."

Finnbar clapped and flashed Gina a reassuring smile. "See, Gina? There are more suspects. Ones with much better motives for murder than your ghost."

Gina twisted her lips, clearly giving the theory some consideration.

Lacey, on the other hand, was giving Finnbar's suggestion more than just a bit of consideration. She cast her mind back to the Halloween party at the Lodge and the creepy vibes Eldritch had given off when he'd stared at her at her through the flames incinerating the Violet Jourdemayne effigy. In fact, he'd given her such a bad feeling, she'd ended up having a nightmare about him. She knew it wasn't just prejudice on her part; none of the other spooky out-of-towners had sucked away her desire to dance to the "Monster Mash" quite like Eldritch Von Raven had. Were her instincts trying to tell her something?

She underlined Eldritch's name on her list. She had a brand new prime suspect.

"Eldritch is staying at the Lodge with the others, isn't he?" she said, tapping her pen on the paper as she mulled over her next steps.

"I'd imagine so," Finnbar said with a nod. "I can't picture any of them choosing to stay at Carol's B&B. Can you?"

Carol's was the other B&B in Wilfordshire, painted Barbie pink on the outside, and filled with flashing neon signs and flamingo statues on the inside.

"No," Lacey agreed. "I don't think any of Eldritch and his crew would set foot in there."

She put her pen down with finality and swiped up her car keys.

"Come on, Chester," she said, whistling to her companion. "Let's go visit Aunty Suzy."

Her dog came trotting to her side, wagging his tail with excitement at the prospect of an adventure.

Lacey headed for the door. "Finnbar, can you do some research on the grimoire for me? I don't know if it's relevant or not, but all the goths came to town because of it, so there might be some clues there."

"I'm on it," Finnbar said, turning immediately to the laptop.

She reached the door and tugged it open. A gust of frigid cold wind blasted inside; the temperature had dropped considerably since a little while earlier.

"Lacey," Gina called. "I know you think I'm a silly fool for believing in the curse, but the truth is none of us really knows, do we? None of us can say for certain what's going on in this crazy cosmos, whether there are ghosts or spirits among us. So just... be careful, okay?"

Lacey didn't know whether it was the cold chill that had gusted into the store, or Gina's warning, but a shiver went right up her spine.

"I will," she said, before hurrying away.

*

The Lodge was bustlingly busy as Lacey entered through the foyer doors and into the wide corridor where the mahogany reception desk was located. The spooky decorations had been pared down a little now the party was over, but there were still enough about the place for actual Halloween day, which had not yet commenced.

Lacey found Lucia on duty today. Her hair was still faintly red from where she'd dyed it for her rag-doll costume, though her usual glossy brunette locks were starting to return. She looked up from her task and her eyes brightened as she registered Lacey and Chester standing in front of her.

"Hi, you guys!" she said, enthusiastically. "Are you here to see Suzy? Because I'm afraid you just missed her. She just got called into the station to give a statement about Alaric." She grimaced. "Horrible business, isn't it? Imagine going on vacation and dying?" She shook her head. "It's just so tragic."

"His friends must be cut up," Lacey said, steering the conversation down the route her investigation wanted her to go.

"I guess," Lucia said. She lowered her voice. "It's hard to tell though since none of them smile anyway. I mean, they literally arrived looking like a funeral procession, so not a huge amount has changed."

"I'm surprised they didn't all check out this morning and leave," Lacey said, leadingly.

"I guess they all want to be together to support one another," Lucia suggested.

Lacey hadn't considered that possibility. Maybe they weren't sticking around because of the grimoire like Taryn suggested, but because of each other? Not that that was the purpose of Lacey asking the question. She'd been trying to get confirmation that Eldritch and his creepy companions were indeed still occupying rooms at the Lodge. By the sounds of things, they were.

"So when are they due to leave?" Lacey asked.

This time, Lucia hesitated. "I—I'm really not meant to give out details about guests."

"Oh, of course," Lacey replied, breezily, to mask her true intentions. She quickly conjured a cover story. "It's just that I was hoping to hold a little Thanksgiving soiree in the Drawing Room. But if you're still hosting all those goths, there probably won't be much space, right?"

"Oh!" Lucia said, looking a little sheepish. "I'm so sorry, I totally forgot you Americans have another holiday to celebrate between Halloween and Christmas." She blushed as she grabbed a blue binder and began flicking through the pages. "Hmm… you know, looks like all the rooms will be fully booked around Thanksgiving. It says here a family from Utah is visiting." She chuckled. "Must be a big family if they've booked the entire Lodge!"

"Will there be any space between when the goths check out and the Utah people check in?" Lacey asked.

Lucia checked the binder. "Yes… if you don't mind celebrating early, there's a couple days free?"

"Perfect!" Lacey said. "I'll go check with Ash and see if he knows how to make Apple Cider Mimosas. They're a family tradition."

She flashed Lucia an easygoing grin and headed off toward the Drawing Room.

Her forced smile fell as soon as she was out of sight. She hated fibbing, especially to someone who'd only ever been kind to her, but it wasn't the worst lie she'd ever told. Besides, she quite liked the idea of hosting a Thanksgiving soiree with her English friends, now that she'd thought of it. She was always learning about their traditions, so maybe it would be nice to introduce them to some of her own. Perhaps if she managed to get this case sewn up in time, she'd actually hold a Thanksgiving celebration.

Chester kept close to Lacey's legs as she entered the Drawing Room. It was more or less empty, with just a couple of older guests sitting in the big red leather armchairs beside the fireplace sipping tea while they quietly read newspapers.

Ash the mixologist was behind the big wooden bar, cleaning glasses. He smiled cordially as Lacey approached.

"Good afternoon," he said politely, slinging the cloth over his shoulder. "Did you come back for that Diabolical Daiquiri you weren't able to drink the other night?"

"I wish," Lacey replied. "But I think it might be a tad too early in the day for hard liquor."

Ash chuckled. "So what can I do for you? Coffee? Tea?"

"Actually, I have a slightly odd request," Lacey said, resting her elbows on the polished mahogany. "I'm thinking about organizing a Thanksgiving soiree. I was considering hosting it here and wanted to know whether I could make a special drinks menu for the night."

The Thanksgiving cover story had worked so well with Lucia, Lacey figured she may as well keep running with it.

It was a good call on her part; Ash's eyes sparked with excitement. He seemed as enthusiastic about cocktails as she was about antiques.

"Sounds great," he said with a grin. "I'd love to help. What did you have in mind?"

"Errr… Apple Cider Mimosas," Lacey blurted, choosing the first thing that popped into her mind, since her family didn't actually have a traditional Thanksgiving cocktail. "Do you know how to make them?"

"Nope," Ash replied. "But I can learn." He twiddled the ends of his waxed moustache. "When will it be?"

"So, Lucia said there might be some quiet time before the people from Utah arrive and after the goths check out." She lowered her voice. "Not that I have anything against the goths being here, I just don't think there'd be enough space for all of us, you know? I'm assuming they drink in here."

Ash laughed. "Only from noon till night."

"Is that so…" Lacey said. "Except for last night, though, right? I distinctly remember them saying they were going to go on the ghost tour the night of my auction. You know, the one on the island with the medieval ruins?"

Ash just shrugged. "They were here, so I guess they changed their mind about the ghost tour. And good thing, too." He leaned across the bar and spoke conspiratorially. "One of them was murdered."

"I heard," Lacey whispered back. "I'm surprised they didn't all check out and flee the second the news broke. I don't think I'd want to stick around in the town my friend got killed in."

Ash opened his mouth to continue gossiping, but instead his eyes went over Lacey's shoulder and he coughed in his throat.

Immediately, the hairs on the back of Lacey's neck stood up. She straightened up, turning slowly to see none other than Eldritch Von Raven himself standing in the doorway.

CHAPTER EIGHTEEN

Lacey gulped. Out of the corner of her eye, she noticed the elderly couple on the couch flashing wary looks at the willowy man in his silky black suit standing in the doorway, before quickly folding up their papers and swiftly exiting the room. Lacey half wished she could scarper too.

If their behavior caused Eldritch any level of discomfort, he didn't show it in his demeanor. Without hesitation, he crossed the Drawing Room to the bar, his black shiny brogue clicking on the floorboards. Chester emitted a low growl as Eldritch halted beside Lacey and rested his pale hands on top of the bar, spreading his long, knobby fingers. His skin, Lacey noted, was exceptionally pale.

"Whiskey on the rocks," he said to Ash.

The mixologist gave him a meek nod and scurried away to make his drink, leaving Lacey and Eldritch alone at the bar together. Eldritch's gaze slid over to Lacey. "I was wondering when you'd show up."

A bolt of anxiety went straight through her. She raised her gaze to meet his, and a chill went up her spine.

"You were expecting me?" she asked with a gulp.

"Of course," Eldritch replied. "I tried to warn you about the grimoire, but you didn't listen. You were greedy and chose to profit from it. Your greed unleashed the grimoire's curse. A man is dead. Now here you are, like a lost little lamb seeking my guidance."

Lacey's mouth dropped open. Of all the arrogant, rude things to say!

"Are you suggesting the curse only struck because I didn't sell it to you?" she exclaimed.

"I'm more than suggesting it," Eldritch said, haughtily. "I am outright saying it. Your audacity at trying to profit from the grimoire has angered the spirits."

Lacey raised an eyebrow. "So put another way... if I'd sold the grimoire to you on the cheap when you'd offered, a man wouldn't have been murdered? Do you have any idea how suspicious that makes you sound?"

It was almost laughable. If Superintendent Turner was here, he'd probably find a way to twist that into a confession and arrest him on the spot.

"I've no need to worry about your suspicions," he replied haughtily. "I was at the Lodge the night Alaric died and there are plenty of witnesses to vouch for me." He nodded his head at Ash.

The mixologist had been watching the encounter out of one eye as he prepared Eldritch's drink. He passed it across the bar to him.

"It's true," he said, looking slightly meek to be siding with the strange gothic man over his actual acquaintance. "He was here drinking with the others all night."

"See," Eldritch said triumphantly.

"There's nothing to be so smug about," Lacey contested. "A man is dead. Murdered."

"Actually, I don't believe he was murdered," Eldritch replied. "Murder can only be committed by corporeal beings. It is a physical act one man does unto another. What happened to Alaric was supernatural."

"If you say so," Lacey replied. She was getting annoyed with all this stuff now. All this silly talk.

"You don't believe me?" Eldritch said, with an arrogant smirk on his lips. "This isn't the first time someone's been harmed by the grimoire. History is littered with examples of prior encounters ending disastrously. Broken bones."

Lacey thought about the pawnbroker and his broken foot. No. It was just a coincidence.

"Well, Alaric got a whole lot more than a broken bone, didn't he?" she challenged.

"Quite," Eldritch replied thinly. "He got a broken neck."

Lacey winced.

"It's the first life the grimoire has taken, as far as I am aware," Eldritch added.

"So whatever ghostly spirit is haunting it, they're escalating?" Lacey replied.

Eldritch looked nonplussed as her quip. "You don't believe in the curse, do you?"

Lacey shook her head. "No. I don't. I believe Alaric was killed by a real person. A flesh and blood killer."

"How can you be so sure? Who knows what hex your colleague said when she read from the book?"

Lacey had reached the end of her patience. She'd got what she came here for anyway—Eldritch had an alibi for the night of the murder. He wasn't her killer.

But who was?

Or was the actual question… what was?

CHAPTER NINETEEN

With Eldritch Von Raven alibied up, Lacey returned to the store. She found Finnbar at the laptop where she'd left him, only now he was surrounded by scribbled notes.

"What happened to you?" she asked.

He startled. "Lacey! I've been reading all about the grimoire. It's fascinating."

"And when was the last time you looked away from the computer screen?" she asked.

He turned his eyes up to her. They were bloodshot. "Now."

Clearly he'd taken the task she'd set him very seriously.

She went around to the counter to join him.

"What happened with Eldritch?" he asked.

"Another dead end," Lacey said with a shake of the head. "But maybe let's not tell Gina that just yet."

"Don't worry, she's in the greenhouse singing to the zucchini."

"Of course she is," Lacey replied. "So, what did you find out about the grimoire?"

She'd already researched the grimoire once in her attempt to value it for the auction, but she knew Finnbar, as a PhD student, was far more adept at research than she.

"It was tough, but I did manage to find mention of it in a few medieval history journals," Finnbar began. "These are scholarly articles. Reputable ones. Peer reviewed."

"I trust your sources," Lacey said, giving him the floor.

"So the book was written in medieval France, as we know," Finnbar said. "He sounded like he was giving a presentation in a lecture theater. "Its precise actual origins aren't known, but it's unanimously attributed to the Ouvrière family. Ouvrière is an occupational surname. It means day laborer. We're talking dirt poor, odd job workers, right at the bottom of the societal ladder."

"Social misfits?" Lacey offered.

"Right. The sort of people who got scapegoated as witches."

"Laborers by day, witches by night," Lacey said.

He nodded. "Pretty much. The Ouvrière daughters were all herbalists, purported to be able to treat infertility problems. The grimoire is thought to be a collaborative effort between them. Some theorize it's essentially just a bunch of aphrodisiac potions, others say it's a spell book full of prayers to the devil."

"I think we know which one the goths believe," Lacey said. "Seventy thousand pounds is an awful lot to spend on a book of aphrodisiacs. Oysters are much cheaper."

Finnbar smiled at her joke. "Anyway, I couldn't find any actual records of what happened to the Ouvrière family, but the two most commonly held opinions are that they were either all executed during the witch trials, or that they managed to flee France in time. The fact the grimoire turned up here in England seems to suggest the latter, wouldn't you agree?"

Lacey nodded as she let the information sink in. No wonder the grimoire had been such a lure to Alaric, Eldritch, and their esoteric entourage. And no wonder she'd felt such a pull to it herself. She'd practically felt the grimoire's complex history when she'd first held it in her hands. Now she knew why. It had been smuggled across the channel on a rickety old medieval boat by young women fleeing persecution. The thought made Lacey tingle all over. To be poor and persecuted to the point you're forced to flee your home country was chilling.

"Did you find out anything about the... curse?" She whispered the final word, just in case Gina had happened to finish singing to her zucchinis and had come up behind her without her knowledge.

"Nothing concrete," Finnbar replied. He checked his notes and read from them. "Suspected to contain long-lost secrets of witchcraft. Considered a collaborative effort between several witches. Potentially imbued with their powers." He peered back at her. "Blah blah blah."

"Eldritch said that word of the book had spread around their inner circle quickly," Lacey said ponderously. "How do you think they passed the message on to one another? How do people in a really niche subgroup even talk about this stuff?"

Finnbar was a bit of a geek. His interests were pretty niche in Lacey's opinion. If anyone would know, it would be him.

"Forums," Finnbar said. "Chat rooms. There'll be some obscure little pocket of the internet somewhere where they all congregate."

"Any idea where?" Lacey asked. If she could find out which dark corner of the internet the group occupied, maybe she could find some incriminating conversations between them, and broaden her suspect list.

"There are millions of host sites," Finnbar said. "For all we know, they could have their own private forum."

"Darn," Lacey said. "I'm guessing a private forum wouldn't be possible to trace?"

Finnbar shook his head. "Unfortunately, no. And I've already searched for all their names from the auction list. The only hits I got were social media profiles and business profiles. If they're posting publicly anywhere, they're using nom de plums."

"That's a shame," Lacey said. She let out a sigh. "But thanks for all this, Finnbar. It's really helpful. I can take it from here."

She headed into her office and began her own research. She combined different key words from the information Finnbar had accumulated and hit the jackpot with *Jourdemayne + curse + grimoire.*

Maybe I should be the PhD student, she thought, clicking the link.

It was an article, or opinion piece might be a better description, on a rudimentary website entitled *Pagan Ponderings.* The article was all about the trial of Violet Jourdemayne for witchcraft. Right at the end, Lacey saw the following:

The key piece of evidence—a spell book supposedly full of incantations to the devil—was never, in fact, found. Scholars have long since debated whether spell books like the one that damned Violet Jourdemayne to her gruesome execution ever really existed, or whether they were merely workbooks, mis-attributed by sexist prosecutors who refused to believe women could be intelligent.

The article was signed off with: *Madeleine Jourdemayne.*

Lacey thought about what Finnbar had said about the goths using nom de plums. The Jourdemayne part of the author's signature was clearly chosen in homage to her favorite witch. But if Madeleine was her actual first name, what were the chances it was the same Madeleine who'd won the ram's skull at the auction, the polite goth girl with the purple lips and hair, whom Gina had been so taken with?

Lacey scrolled down to the comments section. There was a space for visitors to add a comment. She quickly typed.

Are you the same Madeleine I met the other day at the auction in Wilfordshire? I have some questions about curses. I'd love to talk to you about this fascinating subject.

She hit send, and the message posted itself at the top of the comments section.

Suddenly, a voice came from behind her shoulder, making her jump.

"You DO believe in the curse!" Gina cried.

She was as shrill as a banshee. Lacey spun in her chair, her heart catapulting into her throat.

"Jeez! Gina! You scared the living daylights out of me," Lacey said to her friend, clutching her chest.

Gina ignored her and pointed at the screen. Lacey's message about the curse was displayed in stark black and white.

"You do think I unleashed a curse," she said in a small voice.

"No I don't," Lacey said firmly. "I'm just using this as a way to break the ice. To lure her in."

"Lure in who?" Gina asked, squinting. When she saw the name Madeleine Jourdemayne, she drew back and looked perplexed. "Madeleine? From the auction?"

"I think so," Lacey said. She turned back to the screen and scrolled back up the article. "I think she might be the author of this. It's attributed to Madeleine Jourdemayne. Seems pretty likely it's her, don't you think? There can't be many Violet Jourdemayne fans named Madeleine in existence."

"Oh, it's definitely her," Gina replied, with a nod. "We spoke at the auction. Jourdemayne is her real, legal surname. She's a living relative of Violet's."

Lacey's eyebrows shot up her forehead.

"You're kidding me," she said. "That's kind of crazy. Are you sure?"

Gina shrugged. "That's what she told me. But then again, who knows who to trust anymore."

She walked away, worrying her hands in front of her as she went, her mind quite clearly consumed with thoughts of curses and evil spirits. And Lacey had to admit that she, too, was starting to lose the ability to shake off her spooky feelings. This whole case was getting to her. If she didn't solve it soon, she might just lose her mind.

She needed support, someone to make her feel better. And there was only one person who could soothe Lacey in her times of distress. Tom. She stood up from the computer and left.

CHAPTER TWENTY

Lacey opened the door into Tom's patisserie, finding the place as busy as usual, packed with happy children munching on spooky-shaped gingerbread cookies. Their happiness seemed jarring with just how on edge she was feeling.

Chester kept close to her legs as she went to the counter, where Tom's assistant, Emmanuel, was on duty.

"Hello, Lacey," he said when he spotted her. "Tom's out back."

"Thanks," she said, heading for the kitchen.

"Oh, Lacey," Emmanuel said, making her pause in her tracks. "Just for the record, I don't believe what people are saying. I believe you had nothing to do with that man's death."

He put a hand on his heart and smiled his pearly-toothed smile. He was obviously trying to comfort her, but the reminder that people were whispering behind her back and pointing the finger of blame in her direction was not a welcome one.

"Thanks," she mumbled.

The patisserie's kitchen was bright and warm, and smelled deliciously of almonds. Lacey sniffed the gorgeous scent as she glanced around for Tom. Chester ran ahead through the metal shelves searching for him, before they discovered him in the middle of creating a large fruit basket out of marzipan.

"Wow," Lacey gushed. "This is incredible!"

Tom ruffled Chester's head, then looked up and smiled warmly at Lacey. "Thank you, my dear. It's for Ippledean's Harvest Festival fete. They have a squash competition, and commission me to make one of these every year as part of the winner's prize. It's also a pretty good way of drumming up extra business." He kissed her cheek. "And how are you?"

Considering he was in such a chipper mood, Lacey guessed he was clueless as to that morning's events.

"You haven't heard?" she asked.

Tom frowned. "Heard what?"

114

"Superintendent Turner made me a suspect. He came by this morning with a search warrant. Made quite a spectacle of it, too."

Tom looked perturbed. He took her hand and led her to a stool. Chester stuck close by, ever protective, before sinking down at her feet in his Sphinx pose.

"What reason on earth do they have to suspect you?" Tom asked, fixing his earnest green eyes on her.

"The grimoire was stolen," Lacey admitted with a heavy exhalation. "So the cops turned up at my store to search for it. Obviously it wasn't there. The closest they got was the complete works of Shakespeare. But it doesn't matter. Everyone thinks I had something to do with Alaric's murder now."

"Oh, Lacey," Tom said. "I'm so sorry. What are you going to do?"

"I'm going to find out who killed him?" she said confidently. "After all, the only person who's actually motivated to clear my name is me."

Tom flashed her a proud smile. In the past, he'd worried about her penchant for sleuthing, fearing she'd one day find herself in too deep. But he seemed to have finally accepted his future wife wasn't the type to take things lying down.

"Let me guess," he said. "You've already drawn up a list of suspects?"

"Not quite," Lacey said. "But I have questioned the two most obvious suspects."

"You questioned two people already?" Tom said with a whistle. "It's not even lunch time. You have been busy!"

"I figured the quicker I solve this, the more of my reputation I'll walk away with intact," she explained.

"So what did you find out?" Tom asked.

"Well, both my lead suspects had alibis. Jeff Peters was getting his broken foot attended to in the hospital, and Eldritch Von Raven was drinking in the Drawing Room at the Lodge with the rest of his porcelain pals."

"Eldritch Von Raven?" Tom echoed, raising his astonished eyebrows. "What a name."

"He's one of the out-of-towners," Lacey explained. "He was at the Halloween party with the others. He went out of his way to try and circumvent the auction and buy the grimoire off me outright, so I figured he had the most compelling motive."

"And the other guy? Jeff Peters? Why was he on your list?"

"He's the pawnbroker from The Ducking Stool. He was the one who you overheard yelling at me after the auction."

"Ah," Tom said with a nod of understanding. "I see why you made him a suspect."

"Exactly," Lacey said. "But they both have alibis for the night of the murder. Which leaves me with nothing." She felt her shoulders slump with frustration. "Gina's theory that it was the curse that killed him is starting to look pretty plausible."

Tom gave his head an exasperated shake. "Is she still going on about the curse? She can't really believe a supernatural force killed Alaric?"

"She can and she does. And until I work out what really happened, she's going to keep blaming herself."

Tom rubbed his chin contemplatively. "So who's next?" he asked. "Who's your next prime suspect?"

Lacey sighed. "That's where I'm stuck. No one obvious is jumping out at me now I've cleared Jeff and Eldritch, so I've no choice but to completely widen the net and look into every single person who came to the auction and bet on the grimoire. They all have a motive, technically speaking. I'll question every single last one of those vampires if I need to."

Tom bestowed a kiss onto the crown of her head. "Good luck."

Fueled with motivation, Lacey stood. Chester jumped to attention, and together they headed from the back kitchen into the dining area of the patisserie. A large group of youngsters had entered while she'd been out back, and they were all crowded together in between the tables, blocking the route out. Lacey waved goodbye to Emmanuel and began to maneuver her way through. Chester was doing a much better job of it, weaving seamlessly between their legs almost unnoticed.

As Lacey inched a path through the kids, her attention was caught by a poster on the wall. It was the ghost tour poster, the one that had been hanging beside her auction poster during the Halloween party. Curious to know when the tour was actually taking place, she searched for the date.

To her surprise, she saw that Gina had been right about the date all along. The ghost tour *was* supposed to take place the night of her auction. The night of Alaric's murder. Gina hadn't messed up the dates after all.

Her mind flashed back to the beach. When she, Tom, Gina, and the dogs had congregated on the beach at the correct meeting spot, they'd been the only ones there. She knew for certain they weren't the only ones who'd planned to attend the event, and Gina had told her the tour was a highlight of the town's calendar.

The only explanation was that the operators had cancelled the event. She and her crew hadn't bought tickets in advance, instead choosing to pay at the door, so to speak. If the event had indeed been cancelled there would've been no way for the organizers to contact them to let them know, since they hadn't supplied any contact information. That would explain why the beach was empty when they arrived, if everyone else had prebooked and gotten the memo it was cancelled.

Lacey pondered it, not quite knowing what—if any—significance the cancelled ghost tour held. But it had to mean something. The location of Alaric's murder should've been swarming with visitors and tourists had the tour gone ahead. His killer wouldn't have had a chance to strike, and the man would most likely still be alive today. Lacey needed to know why the tour had been cancelled. It might well be the key to unlocking this whole case.

Determined, Lacey rushed out into the street and back toward her store.

CHAPTER TWENTY ONE

Lacey hurried back to the antiques store. It felt even more quiet after the bustle of Tom's patisserie.

"Where's Gina?" Lacey asked Finnbar. He was sitting behind the counter with his nose in one of his big PhD textbooks.

"Out in the greenhouse," he replied. "Singing to the zucchini. Again." He put the book down. "I'm starting to worry about her."

"Don't," Lacey said. "I'll handle her."

She headed through the auction room and out into the garden. She spotted Gina inside the greenhouse, swaying side to side on a stool beside a large zucchini plant as she sang a mournful little ditty. Boudica slept beside her feet.

She really did make for a forlorn figure.

Lacey knocked on the glass window. Gina flinched and turned around.

"Oh. Lacey," she said. "I didn't see you there."

Lacey stepped inside the greenhouse. It was warm and smelled comfortingly earthy.

"How's your zucchini?" she asked.

"Just in need of a bit of company," Gina replied.

Lacey gave her friend a sympathetic smile. "I'm sorry you're going through so much at the moment, Gina. And I know reassuring you there's no such thing as a curse isn't going to help. Is there anything I can do?"

Gina shook her frizzy gray hair and looked over the rim of her glasses. "There's only one thing that can take this load from my mind—proof that someone killed Alaric. Until then, I won't be able to stop thinking that I caused all this."

Lacey felt even more compelled to solve the case for her dear friend.

"Then I'll just have to find that proof for you," she said with determination. "And maybe you can help."

"Oh?"

"I've been thinking about the ghost tour," Lacey said. "I just found out you were right about the date all along. The tour must've been cancelled earlier in the day, but we didn't find out because we didn't have tickets. Do you know who runs it?"

"Jens," Gina told her.

"Jens Johansson?" Lacey asked, surprised. "From the Coffee Nook?"

"Yes, that's right," Gina said. "You seem surprised."

"I am," Lacey told her. "I assumed the tour would be run by a born and bred Wilfordshire local. A Violet Jourdemayne obsessive."

Gina gave her head a small shake. "Nope. Jens tried his hand at a lot of odd jobs when he first moved here from Denmark. The ghost tour stuck. It's probably thanks to the tour that he was able to open the Coffee Nook, and support his sister and her family to move over here too."

Lacey gave the new information a moment to percolate. It didn't fit in with her perception of the calm and intelligent Jens Johansson, being an odd-jobs man. But that was often the way with economic migrants. Jens could have a PhD in molecular science and he'd still be expected to graft his way back up from the bottom, just like Lacey herself had with her antiques store.

She thought back to that morning in the Coffee Nook, when Freja had been dressed as a Teletubby and fudged Alaric's order. Lacey herself had been enraged by the man screaming at a heavily pregnant woman and had stepped in to intervene. Was it possible that when Jens heard about the abusive treatment of his beloved sister, he'd snapped? Perhaps Alaric turned up for the ghost tour early, and Jens had seen red, rowing him out to the island alone to murder him. Why else would Jens have cancelled his lucrative ghost tour, one that was only growing in popularity as the years passed?

Lacey could hardly believe it herself, but she had a new prime suspect. Jens.

She hurried for the greenhouse exit.

"Where are you going?" Gina queried.

"I've had an idea," Lacey said. "Mind the store for me, please. I've got a suspect to question."

And with that, she hurried away.

*

119

Lacey opened the door to the Coffee Nook, and stepped inside the small store. Jens was on the till today.

"Lacey," he said in his soft Danish accent. "How lovely to see you."

He must've been the only person in town who wasn't annoyed at her for luring all the goths here. His lack of irritation only served to make her more suspicious.

"No Freja today?" she asked.

He smiled. "She's at home resting up with the baby."

Despite her reason for being here, Lacey couldn't help but feel a surge of excitement. "She had the baby?"

"Yup. Take a look."

Jens showed her his cell phone. It was full of pictures of a frazzled but happy-looking Freja in a hospital bed, cradling the pink wriggly newborn. In some of the photos, her small daughters were also squidged up beside her posing for a family snap. In others, Freja's husband was present. In others, Jens had used selfie mode to get the whole gang in together. They were joyous images. Images that showed a loving and united family enjoying one of life's most precious moments. Not exactly the types of pictures you'd expect from a murderer.

"She's calling him Carl," Jens said proudly. "And get this funny coincidence. He weighed seven pounds, two ounces, and was born at two minutes past seven!"

Lacey suddenly realized something. "He was born during the ghost tour?"

Jens laughed. "Yes. Typical, huh? The day I make the most money out of the year, and I have to cancel because my sister goes into labor. I don't care though. My nephew is worth so much more than I would've earned that night!"

Lacey let it all sink in.

"Were you already down on the beach when you got the call?" she asked.

If Jens had been down there early setting everything up, there was still a slim chance he'd murdered Alaric before getting the call from Freja. Of course that would've relied on Alaric also being early, and Jens being such a psychopath he was able to murder a man before driving his laboring sister to hospital, but stranger things had happened…

120

"Luckily, no," Jens replied. "It would've been so embarrassing if I'd had to cancel on the spot. As it was, I got the chance to contact everyone who'd prebooked and offer a new date or a refund. Most of them went for the refund, since they're out-of-towners."

Lacey hadn't prebooked. If she had, she would've gotten a call from Jens about the cancellation. She would never have been down on the beach that night, would never have gone to the island, and would never have been embroiled in this whole mess.

So that was that. Jens had an iron-cast alibi. He wasn't her guy. She'd hit another dead end.

CHAPTER TWENTY TWO

Lacey returned to her quiet store. Finnbar was at the desk, looking at the computer.

"Lacey, you should take a look at this," he said.

She went over and peered over his shoulder. He was on the *Wilfordshire Weekly* website. A large photograph of Alaric Moon filled the screen, beneath the headline: "Wilfordshire Wakes to Mysterious Murder of Spooky Stranger."

Lacey groaned at their sensationalism. "At least they're good at alliteration."

"Did you know Alaric ran his own occult museum in London?" Finnbar said. He read from the screen. "The Macabre Museum, it's called. I looked it up. It's not a museum in the traditional sense of the word, it's a business. I wonder if that's why Alaric wanted the grimoire in the first place. To display at his museum. That might explain why and how he was willing to shell out so much for it, if it was a business expense he could write off for tax purposes. I mean, you saw how many people were lured to Wilfordshire because of it. Think of all those people paying an entrance fee to get inside Alaric's museum to look at it. He'd turn quite a profit with the grimoire on display."

"You're right," Lacey said. "That makes a lot of sense."

It didn't get her any closer to solving Alaric's murder, but it certainly helped build up a picture of the man he'd been when he was still alive, the life he'd led, and his interests and motivations. She wasn't sure whether it would prove useful in the future, so she filed the information away in her mind.

"Thing is, Lacey," Finnbar added. He bit down on his lip nervously and scrolled through the article, then began to read from it. *"The man was murdered after attending an auction and putting down a huge sum of money on an antique spell book that was in fact a fake."*

Lacey's eyes widened with alarm.

"A fake?" she repeated. "What do they mean? I mean it's obviously not full of actual spells that work, but it's definitely an antique."

"Keep reading," Finnbar told her.

"Jeff Peters of the Ducking Stool pawn store in Ippledean has confirmed the book was a replica, and was purchased from his store for twenty pounds. However, it was then sold on fraudulently as the real thing, for an exorbitant fee of seventy thousand pounds."

Lacey clenched her hands into fists. "That nasty little man! What a terrible thing to do. And there was me feeling sorry for him!"

Finnbar swirled in his stool to face her. "People are going crazy about it online. They're calling your entire business into question. I've been getting calls all day from people who attended auctions in the past asking for evidence their items weren't faked."

"For goodness' sake," Lacey huffed.

This was all getting out of hand. With the *Wilfordshire Weekly* reporting nonsense, things would only get worse for her and the store. She needed to solve this case and fast, before her entire business fell into disrepute.

Just then, her phone rang. She looked down to see it was her mom.

"Great!" she muttered. Just what she needed.

She hurried away into the back office for some privacy and answered the call.

"I've had the most wonderful idea for the wedding," Shirley said as the call connected.

"Oh?" Lacey asked, feeling her heart thumping in her chest.

"A Celtic harp!"

Lacey paused. "Huh?"

"You should get a Celtic harp player. Imagine how ethereal it would be. A forest of spindly trees, a harp player in a gorgeous floaty dress, snow, icicles."

Despite the emotions rolling inside of her, Lacey was suddenly struck by the image her mother had painted. It *would* be beautiful.

"I... love it," she confessed.

"You do? Great! Because I've drawn up a shortlist of harpists, and I've found an excellent forest location. Ashdown forest, in Sussex."

"Sussex?" Lacey repeated. That's where she'd tried to trace her father to, to Rye in Sussex. Thinking of him sent a visceral pain through Lacey's chest.

"Yes," her mom continued brightly, none the wiser. "They have these lodges, like proper wood cabins. You can hire out the hall for the reception, and the separate rooms for guests to stay in, and then everyone heads into the forest for the ceremony. I'll email you the details."

"Thanks," Lacey said, her mind suddenly elsewhere.

"And you'll be thrilled to know that they've already okayed the reindeer," Shirley added.

"Great," Lacey murmured. She wasn't listening anymore.

The call ended.

Lacey couldn't let this sidetrack her. It would be too easy to get wrapped up in thoughts of her father and lose sight of the more pressing need to solve the case. She shook herself, trying to shake off the thoughts.

It was time to make her next move.

"Come on, Chester," she said to her pup. "Let's go."

*

Evening fell, bringing cooler weather with it. The shop had been quiet all day, but Lacey had been rushed off her feet trying to solve Alaric's murder.

She yawned. "Are you ready to go home?" she asked Chester.

He yipped his agreement.

She closed up the store and headed into the cold night, walking along the dark beach with Chester back home.

It was chilly in Crag Cottage, and Lacey realized it was the first night she could light the fire.

She got the fire going, poured herself a glass of wine, and settled into the cream couch.

She felt like her mind was full to bursting. She'd had such a whirlwind of a day, trying to glean as much information about Alaric and the mindset of his potential killer, that she felt like it was now all sloshing around up there in a messy soup. She needed to organize it. Make sense of it.

She grabbed her laptop. The best thing to do would be to get all her ideas out on the page. That was the best way of dealing with things that were overwhelming her.

As her laptop fired up, Lacey noticed the exclamation point that told she had new emails.

She saw one from her mom, marked as "urgent," and entitled *VERY IMPORTANT WEDDING DETAILS MUST READ NOW!!!"*

Lacey was about to open it when she spotted something else.

It was an email from Madeleine, the author of the article Lacey had read about the grimoire. Lacey opened it instead and began to read.

124

It was indeed the same Madeleine who'd attended her auction and won the ram's skull.

The Grimoire was stolen? she asked.

Lacey typed her reply.

Madeleine must've been online, because a moment later, a return email arrived from her.

I think I know who did it.

She'd included her phone number.

Lacey grabbed her cell and dialed it.

"Hello?" came the purple-haired goth girl's timid voice.

"It's Lacey. What do you know?"

"I think it was Eldritch."

Lacey shook her head. "It couldn't be. Eldritch was at the Lodge on the night of the murder. He has an alibi."

"No. He wasn't," Madeleine said, firmly. "Everyone else was, since the ghost tour was cancelled. But Eldritch didn't come."

Lacey thought of Ash, the mixologist, who'd confirmed Eldritch's alibi.

Or had he? All the goth guests dressed in black. They all had black hair. Would Ash really be able to pick out Eldritch specifically over any of the rest of his group?

"But why Eldritch?" Lacey asked. "Why would he kill Alaric?"

"They used to be business partners," Madeleine explained. "They owned a—"

"Museum," Lacey cut in, recalling the *Wilfordshire Weekly* article. "The Macabre Museum in London."

"That's right."

Lacey was stunned. She'd had no idea Eldritch and Alaric had history, that they'd run a business together. A fallout between business partners was a pretty common MO for murder. Had Lacey finally cracked the case?

"What happened between them?" she asked Madeleine. "Why did they fall out?"

"Because Alaric wasn't actually a believer," Madeleine said, sounding disdainful.

Lacey frowned, confused. "What do you mean?"

"He was a fraud," Madeleine said. "He sold fake tarot readings. Conducted fake seances. He even pretended to be a psychic, and gathered quite a following for it, until someone hacked his computer and discovered he'd simply researched his attendees' social media profiles online. He just peddled mystical stuff for the profit, and he didn't earn himself any friends doing it. Eldritch, on the other hand. He's the real deal. He's a true believer. Once Alaric was exposed as a fake, Eldritch quit in order to salvage his own reputation. He opened a competing museum. They were in direct competition. They both wanted the grimoire in their collection."

Lacey couldn't believe what she was hearing. Former business partners turned rivals thrown together into a competition... That was bound to be explosive! All the conditions for murder had been there. That only one man would leave Wilfordshire alive after the auction was almost a certainty.

"Thank you, Madeleine," Lacey said. "You've been really helpful."

With a spark of renewed vigor, Lacey realized Eldritch's alibi wasn't as ironclad and she'd previously believed. Her prime suspect was right back in the frame.

She felt a wave of determination overcome her. It was time to speak to Mr. Von Raven and see just how much he stuck to his story under pressure. It was time to get him to confess.

CHAPTER TWENTY THREE

When Lacey reached the Lodge, she was glad to find Suzy on duty. She'd not had a chance to speak to her last time she was here, relying instead only on Ash the mixologist's account of the night Eldritch claimed to have an alibi.

She hurried over to her friend, Chester trotting at her side.

Suzy must've noticed the crazed look in her eyes, but her own gaze darted furtively from Lacey to the English Shepherd beside her.

"Lacey, what's wrong?" she asked, sounding concerned. "What's happened?"

Lacey spoke rapidly. "I need to know who was here the night of Alaric's death. Check-in logs, or sign-in books. Surveillance footage. Whatever it is you use to keep tabs on who is in or out of the premises, I need to see it."

Suzy's perfectly sculpted brows turned inward in a frown. "Slow down, Lacey. I don't understand what you're asking of me."

Lacey tried to slow her frantically racing mind.

"One of your guests claimed he was drinking in the Drawing Room the night of Alaric's murder," she explained. "But I have reason to believe he's lying."

Suzy's brown eyes widened with astonishment. "Which guest?"

"Eldritch Von Raven."

Suzy looked stunned. She whispered under her breath, "You think he killed Alaric?" Then her voice went up an octave as she added, panicked, "You think I have a murderer staying in my B&B?"

"That's what I need you to help me find out," Lacey told her.

Suzy paced away, looking fretful. Chester tipped his head to the side and let out a whinny of curiosity as the slim young woman walked the length of the red and gold floor runner, turned on the spot, then walked all the way back. Once she reached Lacey, she fixed her big, deer-like eyes on her.

"You do know you're asking me to break staff and guest privacy?" she said, clearly torn by the dilemma Lacey had presented her with.

"I know," Lacey replied. "And I wouldn't ask if it wasn't so important."

Just then, the foyer doors swished open and a couple entered. Lacey and Suzy fell silent. They gave them a polite nod as they passed by and headed into the Drawing Room. A light bulb went off in Lacey's mind.

"Hey," she said to Suzy, as soon as the couple were safely out of earshot. "The Drawing Room is open to the public, isn't it? So showing me the surveillance wouldn't be breaking any kind of law, strictly speaking."

"It's not the law I'm worried about," Suzy replied. "It's the ethics. I don't want to give the Lodge a bad reputation."

"Well, it's either you help me now," Lacey said, "or Superintendent Turner and his band of merry cops come pounding on your door once they finally get up to speed with the investigation. You don't need me to tell you which of those will damage your reputation more."

Lacey hated to put pressure on her friend, but that was the reality of the situation. Superintendent Turner didn't do things by half measures. Once he realized Eldritch's alibi was wobbly, he'd come storming in with a convoy of cops, leaving the impression in the minds of every guest staying at the Lodge that it wasn't a safe place to be.

Her ploy worked. Suzy gave a sharp nod, her quandary solved, albeit under duress.

"Fine," she said. "What do you need?"

"Let's start with the Drawing Room CCTV," Lacey said. "That's where Eldritch claimed he was the night Alaric died."

Suzy took her by the arm. "Come with me."

She led her down the corridor, Chester keeping pace behind them, and into the back offices. Lacey hadn't actually set foot inside these rooms since the renovation work she'd been employed to do months ago. She was surprised to see a state of the art security system inside, quite the upgrade on the rudimentary one that had operated when it was a former care home. Before, the cameras were fixed, mounted at the corners of the room, flicking between views every six seconds. But the new system was far more sophisticated, with roving cameras and multiple concurrent views, covering pretty much every inch of the Lodge—gardens, guest parking lot, staff parking lot, kitchen, dining room, corridors, elevator, reception desk.

Lacey whistled. "That's quite the comprehensive system you've invested in, Suzy."

"It wasn't me," Suzy said, as she took a seat in front of the glowing screens. "Dad had it all installed after the mayor was shot."

Lacey grimaced as she recalled the terrible crime that had taken place in the Drawing Room with a hunting rifle many months ago. Wilfordshire still had a vacuum in its power structure; the beloved Mayor Fletcher's position had not yet been filled.

Suzy began tapping keys.

"The problem with this thing," she said, frowning at the computer screen, "is you need to be a computing genius to actually work it. Dad seems to forget that I run a B&B, not a multimillion-pound stately home. I can't afford a security guard to sit in here twenty-four hours a day monitoring this thing."

She double-clicked on a folder, and it opened up on the computer screen to show it was full of .mpeg files, with numerical file names.

"Aha," Suzy said. "Found the folder. That's a good start."

She began scrolling though. There were thousands of files.

"Aren't you supposed to delete this stuff as you go?" Lacey asked the side of her blue-lit friend's face.

Suzy shrugged. "Probably. But like I said, you need a computer degree to actually operate it. All I do is leave it running in the background in case of emergencies." Her voice dropped sadly.

"Emergencies like this…" Lacey finished for her.

She felt it too, the gravity of the situation she'd found herself in once more. Ever since coming to Wilfordshire, she'd been surrounded by death and disaster. Misfortune seemed to follow her like a bad smell, and she felt overwhelmed by the apparent impossibility of the task ahead of her.

Just then, she felt Chester nudge her palm with his nose. He could always tell when she was getting down and in need of support. It worked. She felt her resolve return.

"How are we going to find the right night?" she asked.

Suzy double-clicked on a file and a black-and-white view of the Drawing Room filled the screen.

"Voila," she said triumphantly.

"This is the night?" Lacey asked, surprised her friend had actually navigated the minefield of data to pinpoint the one she was actually looking for.

"Yup," Suzy said, before adding, "The files are saved in date order."

"Ohh," Lacey said, relieved that her friend didn't have psychic abilities. Considering everything that was going on at the moment with the curse and grimoire, that was the last thing Lacey needed.

"So, what did Eldritch say he was doing specifically on the night Alaric was killed?" Suzy asked, speeding up the footage that had begun at five a.m. in the morning and depicted a totally empty room.

"He said he was in the Drawing Room drinking with his pals," Lacey explained. "Ash confirmed the alibi, but since all the goths look pretty similar from the back, I think he might have mis-identified who was actually there that evening."

Suzy fast forwarded through the footage and the two women stared at it, as various staff members and guests whizzed in and out of the room in high definition.

"There!" Lacey said, pointing at the screen. The goth group had entered. "Slow it down."

Suzy clicked, and the footage returned to a normal pace.

Lacey checked the time flashing at the bottom of the screen. "Seven p.m.," she said aloud.

If Eldritch was with the group as he claimed, it was the perfect alibi, since it was the exact time participants for the boat tour were supposed to be congregating on the beach. The only thing was, Lacey couldn't see him among them...

"He's not there," she said.

"Maybe he comes in later," Suzy suggested.

She sped up the footage again. The Drawing Room was especially busy with guests, and Lacey could easily see how Ash mis-identified the participants of the goth group. She watched as a few more members joined the others, then a couple more, the small group starting to swell and spill over to a second table.

"Is that him?" Suzy said, suddenly, pausing the footage.

Lacey squinted. The willowy Eldritch was indeed strolling into the Drawing Room, in the same black silky suit she'd seen him wear every other time they'd crossed paths. The only difference in his attire were his big black boots instead of the shiny black brogues.

"That's him all right," Lacey said, watching as he joined the others at the table. "But he's thirty-five minutes late."

"Does that give him enough time to kill Alaric?" Suzy asked, swiveling in the chair to face her.

Lacey did the mental math. "Just about. We found Alaric not that long after seven, but he was already cold by then, so had been dead a while."

Suzy grimaced, her face turning pale.

"We need to check more files," Lacey said. "This isn't the definitive proof I need. Thirty-five minutes is enough if he walks right in through the foyer doors and straight into the Drawing Room, but if he goes up to his room first, or to any other place on the premises first, then that gives him more credence. I don't want to go in all guns blazing and accuse him of something if it turns out he just didn't mention having gone to his room first."

"Lacey," Suzy said with a warning edge in her tone. "I only showed you the Drawing Room because it's open to the public, remember? The corridors, stairs, elevator, all that is staff and guests only. It's private. I don't want to be unethical."

"What about the foyer?" Lacey asked.

Suzy narrowed her eyes. She'd clearly reached her personal limit and wasn't going to budge.

"You're right," Lacey said. "I'll go about it the right way. I'm sorry for asking." She turned to Chester. "Come on, boy, let's go."

She heard Suzy's sigh as she left the back office.

Lacey walked the length of the corridor toward the exit, Chester trotting alongside her, trying to think of her next steps. Eldritch's alibi held up—*just*—but it was sitting on even shakier ground than it had before. She desperately needed to test it further, since there was still a small window of time for Eldritch to commit the crime and make it back to the Lodge for his alibi.

There had to be some way of finding the truth out once and for all.

That's when Lacey passed the large reception desk and noticed it was currently unmanned. Lucia was nowhere to be seen. Neither were any of the part-time relief staff she knew Suzy drafted in during busy times.

Lacey peered into the dining hall, looking past the large tables filled with visiting tourists, and spotted Lucia attending to the guests. It looked like she was taking down an order. Lacey realized there must've been a problem with the drafting in of relief staff if Lucia, the manager, was on waitress duty.

Lacey slowed her step. She glanced back over at the vacant reception desk, a plan formulating in her mind.

Chester, noticing the change in pace, looked up at her with his curious brown eyes. His innocent, trusting little face made her feel bad about even thinking what she was thinking. But despite the immorality of it, she realized she had no choice but to do it anyway. She had to catch Eldritch.

CHAPTER TWENTY FOUR

Lacey glanced down the length of the Lodge's main corridor, making sure the coast was clear. Noises of clinking cutlery came from behind the kitchen door, and hubbub radiated from the Dining Hall. It appeared that all the staff were preoccupied by the crowds dining, leaving it wide open for Lacey to enact her plan.

She looked down at her English Shepherd dog waiting patiently beside her feet, and put a finger to her lips.

Right away, Chester's eyebrows twitched upward into what could only be described as an expression of judgment. Even he could tell what she was planning to do was bad.

"Shhh," she said, showing him her flat palm. "Wait."

Chester obeyed her hand gesture by adopting his sentry pose, but he did not look happy about it.

Lacey made a beeline for the unmanned reception desk and darted around the back of it. She rummaged through the stacks of binders until she found the one for room bookings, and opened it up. She scanned the pages, her eyes darting up on occasion to make sure the coast remained clear, her pulse fluttering rapidly as she searched for the name Eldritch Von Raven.

"There," she said when she spotted it. She jabbed her finger at his name. "Room 3."

She was about to return the folder to the pile when the name Alaric Moon jumped out at her. Her curiosity piqued, she scanned the page for a second time, slower to absorb more information.

Alaric had been staying in Room 4, she learned. He was right next door to Eldritch. The two men had been booked into neighboring rooms.

Had that proximity caused them to come to murderous blows? Had the grimoire lured the two old rivals to the same place at the same time, and reignited their bitter feud? Had all the conditions for a jealousy-fueled motive for murder been perfectly laid out?

Lacey shuddered at the thought.

Then, suddenly, she heard a noise from down the hall. She snapped back to the present moment, shutting the folder and shoving it haphazardly beneath the others stacked on the desk. She turned quickly to the vintage wooden key organizer behind the desk.

"Forgive me, Suzy," she whispered under her breath, as she grabbed the little bronze key for Room 3 off its hook and hurried away.

Her heart pounded as she ran over to where Chester was standing guard. She reached him just in time to bump into someone exiting the dining room.

She jumped back in shock, letting out a terrified yelp as her fear ratcheted up a level, thinking she may have bumped into Eldritch. But as she stepped back, she realized she'd collided with Lucia.

"Oof, sorry, Lacey!" Lucia exclaimed. "I didn't see you there. Is everything okay?"

"I'm fine, fine," Lacey replied, her fluttering heart rate returning to normal. She quickly moved the pilfered key behind her back so it was out of sight. "I just popped in to say hi to Suzy but I'm heading off now. It's clearly not a good time; you guys seem rushed off your feet."

"We are," Lucia replied, puffing air out her cheeks. "Let's catch up soon though, yeah?"

She was already walking away, speaking over her shoulder as she headed off down the corridor.

"Sure," Lacey replied. She flashed her a thumbs-up. "Sounds good."

Lucia grinned, then turned and disappeared through the kitchen doors. They swung shut noisily behind her.

Lacey let out the anxious breath she'd been holding.

Just then, she spotted the security camera on the wall opposite the door through which Lucia had just disappeared, and glanced back over at the reception desk. There was another camera there, right up in the corner, blinking a red light and angled down at the desk. Lacey realized her little indiscretion would be discovered sooner or later. All she could do was hope that when she was found out, the ends would justify the means, and a killer would be sitting in jail where he belonged.

She brought the key out from behind her back and glanced over at the staircase. It was a beautiful feature, made of restored, polished beech wood, with a fluffy red velvet floor runner up the center, bordered with gold metal.

"Come on, Chester," Lacey said, heading for them.

Her dog let out a gruff noise and followed reluctantly.

Lacey ascended two steps at a time, ignoring Chester's judgy expression of disdain as he trotted up alongside her. Lacey knew that breaking into someone's room was wrong, and she didn't need her dog to lay the guilt on even more.

She passed a chambermaid heading down the staircase carrying a stack of colorful hand towels, and attempted a pleasant smile. Luckily the girl just smiled in reply as she continued on past. Lacey appeared to not be rousing any suspicion.

She reached the small landing where the door to Room 3 was. Room 4—the one where Alaric had been staying before his murder—was directly opposite. Just a small landing separated the two. It would've taken Eldritch a matter of seconds to cross that space.

She knocked on the dark oak door and listened. Her prepared cover story was that if Eldritch was inside she'd announce she was room service. If he wasn't, she'd use her key to get inside and snoop for clues.

Her knock was met by silence. She tried again. Still nothing.

She put the key in the lock and twisted, then held her breath, anxious over what exactly she might find on the other side—monkey skulls, pentagrams, crystal balls... more dead bodies? She forced the anxious images out of her mind, found her courage, and pressed down on the handle.

She opened the door just enough to peep inside. No monkey skulls. No dead bodies lying on the bed. The room was perfectly neat and tidy, and everything was quiet and still.

She looked back at Chester. "Will you stand guard?"

He whined, sounding thoroughly displeased. Lacey could tell he was not happy with her right now. Maybe assigning him duties was a step too far?

"Fine. You can come inside with me," she relented.

She headed inside the room.

It was the first time Lacey had actually set foot inside one of the Lodge's bedrooms since she'd helped Suzy decorate them all. It felt like a long time ago now, and she was pleasantly surprised to see just how well she'd done designing the place; the wallpaper was a gorgeous replica of the English Spitalfields' silk design from the Regency period, in a lush green color, and was complemented perfectly by the walnut-polished floorboards and sheepskin rug. Interior design was another one of those talents Lacey no longer used, one she'd left behind with the New York City version of herself. She shook the thoughts away. Now was hardly the time.

Eldritch had kept his things quite neat. Lacey found his suitcase in the wardrobe and began to rifle through it.

Clothes. Lots and lots of black clothes. It seemed that was all Eldritch had brought with him, a walk-in wardrobe's worth of black clothes. Didn't he get bored wearing the same color every day?

Just then, her fingers collided with something that wasn't fabric. It felt like paper.

She pulled it out and gasped. It was a page of the Grimoire, torn along the seam. She recognized it immediately by the thickness and greasiness of it, and the off-yellow color.

"Eldritch did steal the grimoire," Lacey said, turning to Chester, waving the paper in the air. "This is evidence!"

Then she stared at the page in her hand. Her triumph began to fade. Because now that she'd confirmed Eldritch was the thief, it stood to reason that he was also the person responsible for the murder of Alaric Moon.

"I was right," she muttered. "Eldritch is the killer."

CHAPTER TWENTY FIVE

Lacey stared at the torn page of the grimoire, her hands beginning to tremble. This was the proof she'd needed to corroborate her hunch that the two men had tussled over the book, leading to Alaric falling from the tower.

She couldn't help but feel responsible. Her auction had drawn the former friends back together. Had the competition over winning the grimoire reignited their long-standing feud? If only she'd just sold the book outright to Eldritch when he'd offered, none of this would've happened.

She began to rummage through Eldritch's closet again, sifting through his piles of black clothing in search of the rest of the book, knowing the whole thing would be stronger evidence than just a single page.

As she worked, Chester watched her. He'd sprawled himself across the sheepskin rug and was following her movements with a very unimpressed expression.

"Come on, Chester," Lacey said over her shoulder. "Why aren't you on my side on this one? I've just found evidence that Eldritch stole the grimoire. That he's the killer."

But no sooner had the words left her lips than Lacey suddenly heard the sound of the door handle being wrenched down from outside.

She flew to her feet and swirled from the closet just as the door swung open inward, revealing the tall, willowy, black-clad figure of Eldritch Von Raven.

Lacey gulped. She'd been caught red-handed.

Eldritch took a beat to survey the scene—Chester on the rug; Lacey by the closet holding his clothing; the dresser drawers hanging open—and an expression of incredulous shock overcame his features. His usually pale white skin inflamed, turning red with fury.

"What the hell are you doing in my room?" he bellowed.

Lacey's heart pounded. She had nowhere to run. Nowhere to hide.

She held up the clothes and heard her excuse come out of her lips in a timid, shaky voice. "Room service?"

Her cover story seemed suddenly obviously inadequate.

Eldritch Von Raven put his hands on his hips and regarded her with a thunderous expression.

"Room service?" he challenged. "Do you really expect me to fall for that? I know who you are!"

Lacey dropped the act. It was a pointless charade to keep up. Of course Eldritch remembered her.

"Fine," she said. "You're right. I'm not here to make your bed. I'm here because of this." She held the page of the grimoire aloft.

There was an instant switch in Eldritch's expression. He went from angry to scared. Lacey immediately knew she was onto something here. Now who was the one caught red-handed?

Feeling emboldened, she spoke. "You stole the grimoire, didn't you?"

Eldritch looked furious at the accusation. "No. I stole a page of the grimoire to send to an authenticator. That's all."

Lacey gave him a look. "You really expect me to believe this is all you took from it?"

"Believe what you want," came his testy reply. "It's the truth. Now will you kindly get the hell out of my room?"

Lacey stood her ground. "Still, it doesn't matter. This is evidence enough. It proves you had contact with the grimoire, that you had your hands on it. It proves you killed Alaric Moon."

Eldritch stared at her, his black eyebrows drawn down together. Then suddenly, he burst out laughing. Deep belly chuckles shook his whole body.

"You think *that's* proof I'm the killer?" he said, scoffing with disdain and nodding at the ripped page in Lacey's hand.

"Besides me, my staff, and Alaric, the only other person who even had the chance to steal a page was his murderer," Lacey said.

Eldritch's lips twitched up into an arrogant smirk. "I stole the page from you. When the grimoire was in your store."

Lacey was taken aback. "W—what?" she asked, dumbfounded. "When?"

"Before the auction," Eldritch explained in a languorous voice like this whole thing was very boring to him. "I came in to try and buy it from you, remember?"

"Of course I do," Lacey replied. "But I was with you the whole time."

"Au contraire," Eldritch drawled. "Your clerk had a little accident with a skeleton. Something to do with a black cat, if I recall correctly. You went to help him and left me alone with it. It was only a brief moment, but it was long enough for me to take the page."

Lacey was stunned. He'd stolen the page while Finnbar had been floundering helplessly underneath the skeleton? How stupid of her to forget she'd left him alone with it!

Suddenly, Lacey started to doubt herself. Her complete confidence that Eldritch was the killer suddenly faltered. If all he was guilty of was tearing a page out of a book, then her breaking into his room was a huge, unjustifiable mistake.

"Now we've cleared up that little misunderstanding," Eldritch said, gesturing to the door behind him, "I will ask you again to kindly get the hell out of my room."

Lacey ground her teeth. She wasn't about to fold that easily. Eldritch might be exuding arrogant confidence in his innocence, but so would any other murderous psychopath in the same situation. They were infamous for their ability to stay calm under pressure and smooth talk their way out of any tricky situation. Lacey had to hold her ground.

"Where is the rest of the book?" she demanded.

"I don't know," Eldritch told her firmly. "Because I am not a thief."

"I beg to differ," Lacey replied. "You admitted to stealing a page from the grimoire. By definition that makes you a thief."

"Oh goody," Eldritch drawled sarcastically. "We're going to engage in a battle of semantics, are we?"

"Yes. And you're a vandal, too, now I think of it," Lacey shot back. "Because you damaged a rare antique."

If there was one thing Lacey had learned in her short amateur sleuthing career, it was that killers hated to be insulted. Especially their intelligence. She could tell Eldritch thought very highly of himself. If she could just worm her way under his skin, perhaps he'd crack.

Indeed, Eldritch seemed to be becoming agitated. He paced away from the door and crossed the floor, letting out a long sigh. "If I'd wanted to steal the entire grimoire, don't you think I would have just done it when the opportunity presented itself to me in your store before the auction?"

"No, I don't," Lacey countered. "Because it would have been far too obvious who took it. Besides, if you'd run out of my store without paying, you wouldn't have gotten very far." She cast her eyes over to Chester. "I have very good security."

Chester puffed up his chest with pride.

"Who said I would've run?" Eldritch shot back, not missing a beat. "Who said I wouldn't have just walked calmly out of the door not rousing the suspicion of your canine whatsoever?"

Lacey shook her head. "You're underestimating his intelligence. Chester knows all the tricks thieves play. Trust me when I say you wouldn't have gotten five paces without him bringing you down."

Eldritch's agitation turned suddenly to fury. "Really? You really think I'd conjure up this elaborate plan to steal the grimoire—and murder a man, no less—just to avoid getting a dog bite?" His tone was incredulous, like he'd never heard anything more preposterous in all his life. He gesticulated wildly to emphasize the point. "You think I'd kill my acquaintance and risk spending my life in jail? *You* are underestimating *my* intelligence! In fact, you are downright insulting it!"

He sank down onto the bed and dropped his head into his hands. His jet black hair splayed across his pale arms like a waterfall of oil.

Lacey regarded him for a moment while his words sunk in. Though she didn't care for the manner in which he'd spoken, he had made a good point. Would he really kill a man, an acquaintance, on an isolated island, just so he could steal the grimoire from the room opposite his own? And then stick around in town long enough to be found out? Doubt suddenly took hold of her.

But just as her faith in herself was beginning to falter, Lacey spotted a pair of Eldritch's boots propped neatly beside the bed. It was the same pair she'd seen him wearing in the CCTV footage, big, black chunky leather. The bottoms and soles were caked in sand. Gray sand. The distinctive color of the sand on the island.

Lacey's heart leapt. That was it. She didn't need the rest of the grimoire to strengthen her accusations, because the sand on Eldritch's boots was more than enough evidence that he'd been to the island the night of Alaric's murder.

Her confidence bolstered, Lacey raced over to the bedroom door, now left unguarded, and clicked the lock shut.

From where he was sitting on the bed, Eldritch's head darted up at the sound of the lock turning.

"What are you doing?" he demanded.

Lacey pulled out her cell phone. "I'm calling the police."

"What?" Eldritch cried. "NO!"

He sprang up from the bed, as if to make an attempt to lunge for the phone. But in the same instant, Chester leapt into action. He bounded across the room and stopped in front of Lacey, adopting a protective stance, his teeth bared. He let out a low snarl at Eldritch.

"I told you I have good security," Lacey said.

With a fearful expression on his face, Eldritch began to back away, his hands held up in a sign of submission. So much for not being concerned about a dog bite, Lacey thought. Eldritch was clearly terrified by the sight of Chester's bared fangs.

"Glad to see you're on my side at last," she muttered to her dog out of the corner of her mouth .

Keeping her eyes on Eldritch, she pressed the phone to her ear.

"Wilfordshire police station," came a voice through the speaker.

"I need the cops," Lacey said. "Now. I know who killed Alaric Moon and I've got him trapped."

CHAPTER TWENTY SIX

From the other side of the window, Lacey heard the sound of tires crunching on gravel. She peeped through the curtain, looking down at the Lodge's parking lot below. Several police cars were rolling in, along with a black riot-squad van.

Lacey grimaced. So much for trying to protect the Lodge's reputation.

"They're here," she told Eldritch, turning back to the B&B room to face him. "And it looks like they brought backup, so I wouldn't try any funny business if I were you."

From where he was sitting on the bed, Eldritch glared up at her. There wasn't much he could try even if he wanted to. They were on the first floor, so jumping out the window would get him a couple of broken legs at the very least, and Chester was guarding the door. Eldritch's only chance of escaping through the door would be if he resorted to physical violence against a dog, and Lacey knew he was smart enough to know who would win that particular fight. Besides, considering he was being accused of a violent murder, attacking a lovable canine wouldn't do much to help his case.

Lacey took another quick glance out the window. The vehicles had stopped, and officers were now jumping down from the open side door of the black riot van.

It was a proper riot squad, she noted, wearing bulky, heavy, black uniforms, with batons in holsters at their hips. She watched them congregate in front of an officer for a briefing, before filtering off in all directions around the sides of the premises.

Lacey realized they were covering all the exits, and presumed that was in case Eldritch attempted to flee. It all seemed rather heavy-handed to her. Yes, he was a murderer, and therefore violently unpredictable, but right now she was doing a perfectly fine job of containing him with little more than the threat of a dog bite. Why Superintendent Turner had decided to send in the riot squad was beyond her.

Speaking of Superintendent Turner…

Lacey peered down at the cop cars, searching for the black Merc driven by the two plainclothes detectives. But it wasn't there. Neither Superintendent Turner nor DCI Lewis were anywhere in sight.

They didn't come, Lacey thought, not knowing what to make of it. It wasn't like them to miss all the fun. At least, it wasn't like Karl. He always made sure he was present for the more dramatic moments of his cases, like searches and arrests. She'd expected to see him for this.

Suddenly, noises erupted from somewhere downstairs. Lacey drew back from the window with a gasp, letting the curtains fall back into place. Her heart leapt as the sounds of shouting came from somewhere downstairs, inside the B&B, along with the clattering of cutlery and shrieks of terror.

The cops were inside.

Lacey looked over at Eldritch, her captive, sitting on the bed with an anguished expression, his bony hands clasped together as the sound of heavy boots thudding on the staircase began. The noise grew louder and louder, closer and closer, until a sudden pounding came at the door, so loud and insistent Eldritch, Lacey, and Chester all started in unison.

"Police!" a male voice boomed. "Open up!"

Eldritch looked up at Lacey. "May I?" he asked, curtly.

She nodded. "Chester," she said, giving a whistle instruction to her dog for him to stand down.

He moved aside, slinking over to Lacey, his gaze fixed suspiciously on Eldritch as the elegant man stood from the bed, moved over to the door, and unlocked it with a click.

The door came flying open with a whoosh. It was so forceful, Eldritch staggered backward and landed on his backside on the bed again. A barrage of officers came crowding into the room, shouting commands as they entered.

"HANDS WHERE I CAN SEE THEM! HANDS WHERE I CAN SEE THEM! HANDS WHERE I CAN SEE THEM!"

Her heart in her throat, Lacey's hands immediately shot into the air. Eldritch raised his hands, too, though he did it in an altogether more nonchalant manner. Chester cowered at Lacey's feet as the room was quickly infiltrated by black-clothed cops.

"We've had reports of a hostage situation," one of the officers announced. "A woman said she was trapped with a killer." He looked at Lacey. "Ma'am, are you hurt?"

Lacey immediately realized what was happening. There'd been a huge misunderstanding. She'd told the operator she'd trapped a murderer, not that she'd been trapped *by* one! No wonder the detectives weren't here; the riot squad had been sent in to defuse what they thought was a kidnapping.

She opened her mouth to explain, but was cut off by Eldritch.

"It's me!" he shouted. "I'm the hostage! This woman broke into my room! Threatened me! Locked me up!"

The officer regarded him skeptically. "The operator said the call came in from a woman."

Lacey opened her mouth for a second attempt at explaining, but she was interrupted again, this time by Suzy, who suddenly appeared in the doorway. Her intrusion prompted a huge, shouted reaction from the officers.

"Ma'am, step back! Step back! We are dealing with a potentially volatile hostage situation!"

"This is my hotel," Suzy declared, furiously. She went up onto her tiptoes, trying to see over the tall officer's wide-set shoulders. "I demand to know what is going on."

Just then, her eyes found Lacey, and her mouth fell open with dismay.

"Lacey!" she cried. "What are you doing in here? I told you to leave! You can't go sneaking into people's rooms!"

"Catching Alaric's killer!" Lacey cried, flinging her arm out toward Eldritch.

The officer's expression became perplexed. He looked from Lacey to Suzy. "I'm sorry, are you saying the woman here is the aggressor?"

Suzy huffed. She looked furious. "Aggressor, no. Pain in my backside, yes."

The energy in the room began to shift, turning from high-octane energy to confusion.

"But then who's he?" the officer asked Suzy, pointing at Eldritch.

"He's a guest," Suzy said. "And this is his room."

"So then who is she?" the officer asked, pointing next at Lacey.

Suzy shot a daggered look at Lacey. "She is my meddling friend."

Guilt began to creep into Lacey. She felt her stomach start to churn. The last thing she'd wanted to do was hurt her friend, but she could see now how she'd gotten carried away with herself. Her high from catching out Eldritch began to ebb away, and she felt herself deflate.

The officer looked back at Lacey. "Ma'am, is this true? Are you trespassing?"

"Yes!" Eldritch yelled.

144

"Now, just hold on one second!" Lacey cried. "There is no hostage situation going on here. I have proof that this man is a murderer. I called the cops, then locked the door to make sure he couldn't flee."

"I'm not a murderer!" Eldritch exclaimed.

The officer ignored his pleas and looked at Lacey. "You locked him in? Against his will? Which would make him, by definition, a hostage."

"Precisely!" Eldritch cried.

"It was a citizen's arrest!" Lacey countered. "Look, wait until Superintendent Turner gets here. He'll understand."

"Superintendent Turner is here," came a booming voice from the door.

Everyone turned toward the six-foot-something man now standing in the doorway. He was wide enough and tall enough to take up the entire frame.

Silence fell.

Lacey couldn't quite believe it, but she was actually happy to see him for once. At least he'd be able to unravel this mess.

His boots thudded on the polished floorboards as he entered. He looked straight at Lacey, his glare burning into her.

"You. Speak. Now," he commanded. "Tell me what the hell I am looking at here."

Finally, Lacey got a chance to properly explain what was going on.

"I realized Eldritch was the killer—"

"—I'm NOT!" Eldritch interrupted.

"—So I locked the door to stop him from fleeing. But my citizen's arrest got misconstrued as a hostage situation, hence all the riot police."

Superintendent was still and silent for a beat, looking like he was absorbing it all. Then he nodded once.

"I want everyone out," he announced.

"Sir, we have orders—" the riot officer began, but Superintendent Turner cut him off with a palm held in front of his face.

"I said everyone out. Everyone but him." He pointed to Eldritch. "And her." He pointed to Lacey. Then his gaze fell to Chester. "And Fido can stay too."

The riot man looked extremely nonplussed by the superintendent's rude hand gesture and tone. With his jaw set firmly, he spoke into the walkie-talkie at his shoulder in a low, indecipherable voice.

The walkie-talkie bleeped, and a voice crackled out, "Affirmative, stand down."

The riot officer's face turned beet red. He clenched his teeth and surveyed the scene.

"Everyone out," he announced.

The officers noisily filed out of the room, leaving Suzy staring openmouthed at the door.

"Please exit the room," Superintendent Turner told her.

"This is my B&B," she protested.

"Then go and do B&B things. This is police business."

And with that he slammed the door in her face.

Lacey grimaced. Suzy was not going to take any of this lightly, and she felt terrible for having instigated all this upheaval. She would have to make it up to her, that much was for certain. Hopefully, once Eldritch was in jail, she'd see that the ends justified the means.

With everyone gone, the room became eerily quiet. Superintendent Turner glanced from Lacey to Eldritch, then pointed at the man.

"You. Speak."

"I'm not a killer," Eldritch said. "Whatever evidence Lacey thinks she has on me, I can explain it."

Superintendent Turner looked at Lacey. "Well?"

"He has a soured business relationship with the victim," she began.

"We parted ways," Eldritch argued. "But there was nothing sour about it."

"He has a page from the missing grimoire."

"Which I ripped out before the auction!" Eldritch exclaimed.

"He gave a false alibi for the night of the crime."

"Nonsense! I was here drinking whiskey with my friends. Ask the mixologist. He'll tell you."

"And then there's the sand on his boots," Lacey added, pointing to the pair by the nightstand.

"I went to the beach, so what?" Eldritch replied. "Doesn't every tourist who visits this town do the same?"

"The sand is gray," Lacey said without hesitation. "Only the sand on the island is that color. Since the beach was a cordoned off crime scene after the murder, the only time he would've been able to visit it was before. Between surveillance footage of him at the Lodge, at the Halloween party, and at my auction, the only possible time he had to be on the island was during the window of Alaric's death. It places him at the location of the crime."

Eldritch faltered. Superintendent Turner's eyebrow twitched up in a subtle expression of triumph and Lacey felt a swell of pride to realize she'd finally proven herself in front of Superintendent Turner.

"Look," Eldritch said. "We were business rivals, that much is true. But there was no real animosity between us. Not really. We pranked each other, that's all. Messed around. I never had any intention of buying the grimoire, I just wanted you to think it was worth that much to screw with him. But I didn't kill him! I knew he was going to the island on the tour, so I rowed over there after the auction. I was just going to spook him. He doesn't really believe in witchcraft, so I wanted to make him realize the grimoire was really cursed. But when I got wind that the tour had been cancelled, I gave up, figuring he wasn't coming to the island after all."

"That," Superintendent Turner said, "is the biggest pile of trite I've heard in my life." He produced his handcuffs from his pocket. "Eldritch Von Raven, aka Richard Bird, I am hereby arresting you on suspicion of murder."

CHAPTER TWENTY SEVEN

From the foyer of the Lodge, Lacey stood shoulder to shoulder with Suzy, watching as Superintendent Turner hauled a cuffed Eldritch Von Raven toward his black Merc.

"I didn't do anything!" the gothic man cried. "I swear!"

Superintendent Turner guided him into the back of the car and slammed the door behind him. He went to the front of the car, gave Lacey a final parting look, nodded once, then disappeared inside behind the tinted black windows of his vehicle.

Lacey felt a swell of triumph and pride. She'd solved the case, and the killer was caught. Everything could go back to normal. Well, once she'd made amends, that was...

She turned to her friend beside her. "I'm really sorry about all that," she said.

Suzy narrowed her eyes. Her lips were pressed tightly together, forming a tight line. "Yes. Well. You do have quite the knack for causing a disruption, don't you? But I suppose having a murderer hiding out in my B&B would've been the greater evil."

"Am I forgiven?" Lacey asked hopefully.

Suzy's lips twitched upward. "Yes, I suppose you are."

Lacey threw her arms around her friend. With Suzy's forgiveness, she could now truly feel elated for having solved the case.

"Just don't do it again!" Suzy warned from the midst of Lacey's embrace.

Lacey let her go. "Oh, don't you worry about that. I have no intention of playing detective ever again. Especially if it's going to cost me my friends."

Suzy gave her a nod, clearly accepting her apology was genuine. "Good. Because your sleuthing will get you in serious trouble one day. And I never want to have to say I told you so."

"I promise," Lacey said.

She pulled up the hood of her coat; a light rain had started to fall. She looked over at Chester. "Come on, boy, I think we should head home and celebrate. And maybe make Aunty Suzy a cake to say sorry…"

Suzy gave her an affectionate eye roll, and Lacey headed through the glass doors into the drizzle.

"Oh, Lacey!" Suzy called after her, as she began to trot down the first stone steps.

Lacey turned and looked back at her friend, lit by the bright, warm, yellow glow of her cozy B&B. "Yes?"

Suzy grinned. "I prefer cinnamon rolls."

Lacey chuckled, relieved to have such understanding friends, and elated that the case that had plagued her was now done and dusted. "Cinnamon rolls. Got it."

And with that, she hop-skipped down the final steps, eager to get back to the others and tell them the good news.

*

"You should've seen Superintendent Turner's face when he realized I'd cracked the case," Lacey exclaimed, swilling the wine in her glass.

She was sitting in the kitchen of Crag Cottage with Tom, Gina, and Finnbar, celebrating having cracked the case. They'd shared a bottle of wine between them. Either Lacey was giddy with joy, or the wine had gone straight to her head, because she felt a tad tipsy.

"I mean, he didn't actually say I'd done a good job," she continued. "But his eyebrow twitched."

"An eyebrow twitch, eh?" Tom said, from the other side of the round kitchen table. "Congratulations."

Everyone chuckled.

Gina yawned deeply. "I'm just glad it's all over. I don't know about you, but thinking you've unleashed an evil curse that killed a man is *exhausting*."

Lacey patted her friend's hand. She was relieved Gina could put this whole curse anxiety behind her at last. Her dear friend had been through quite enough.

"I'm actually kind of sad it's over," Finnbar announced. "I was really enjoying researching the grimoire."

Lacey laughed. Trust the PhD student to come out with such a thing.

149

"Really," Finnbar continued with earnest enthusiasm. "I found out so many fascinating things about it. Once you deep dive the topic, there's all this stuff about the Ouvriere family who supposedly wrote it, and there's this whole legend about how the thirteenth daughter of the thirteenth daughter is a witch, and can invoke Violet's power by sacrificing a charlatan on La Toussaint, which is the French equivalent of All Saint's Day, which is the original pagan holiday that Halloween is derived from." He gasped for air.

"Sounds like it would make a good movie," Tom interjected, before the young man had another chance to launch into yet another monologue.

"Funny you should say that," Finbarr said, "because a movie was made about it in the seventies, but it was banned from being screened by some witchy organization in France that claimed it was slanderous. The film went straight to VHS, flopped, and years later became a cult hit."

Lacey laughed. Trust Finnbar to get so involved in the topic he'd go as far as to research the movie adaptation.

"Ooh, is that the time?" Gina said suddenly. "I'd better head home. Madeleine checked out of Carol's earlier today and will be heading home once she's popped around to say goodbye."

"So one of the goths *did* check in to the Barbie pink B&B after all!" Tom said, surprised.

Lacey smiled at Gina. "It's nice how you two got to know one another. Despite everything that went on, it's nice some good came of it."

"She's a very sweet child," Gina replied. "Shy. Polite. She reminds me of my boy when he was her age."

She smiled a faraway, sorrow-filled smile. Then she put both her palms flat on the tabletop and pushed off. "Right. Thank you for dinner, Tom. Lacey, Finn, I'll see you two bright and early tomorrow."

She waved goodbye and headed out through the stable doors, with Boudica following along.

"I should probably get home too," Finnbar said. "I'll need a lot of energy to take down the store's Halloween decorations tomorrow. Gina told me that you'd only agreed to put them up on the proviso there wasn't a scrap of evidence by November first."

Lacey laughed. "That's quite right."

He gave Lacey his customary head-tip, then repeated the gesture for Tom's benefit, then left.

Lacey settled back into her chair and took a sip of the fruity Shiraz. She glanced over at Tom across the table, lit handsomely by the candlelight, and their eyes met. He smiled at her tenderly.

"Chester must be exhausted," he said, nodding to where the pooch was fast asleep and snoring in his basket by the door. "He didn't even say goodbye to Boudica."

"The riot cops gave him quite a fright," Lacey said. "And he was less than thrilled by me sneaking into Eldritch's room in the first place."

"Him and me both," Tom replied, with a look. "Of all the dangerous things you've done, locking a murderer in a room is quite high on the list."

Lacey glanced down into her wine glass. "I know, my love. But it was worth it in the end, wasn't it? Alaric's killer is in jail. And Superintendent Turner wouldn't have found the smoking gun clue on his own. Only a local like myself would have been able to connect all those dots."

"I still don't understand how you pieced it all together," Tom said.

"It was the boots," Lacey told him. "Or at least the sand on them. You can only pick it up from the island, so it's irrefutable evidence he was there. I saw he was wearing them on the CCTV footage at the Lodge, and there was no other way to explain how it got there. I mean Eldritch—or should I say *Richard Bird*—tried spinning some story about how he only went to the island to prank Alaric but Karl and I saw right through it."

"You and Karl?" Tom teased. "You're not thinking of replacing Beth as his righthand woman, are you?"

"Absolutely not!" Lacey exclaimed, chuckling. "If Alaric's body is the last one I ever see, I'll be happy. But it was pretty thrilling cracking the case. Perhaps in another life, I would've made a good detective."

"Well, if you are planning on swapping careers any time soon," Tom said, standing and collecting the dishes, "just give me a heads-up."

"Will do," Lacey said.

As Tom retreated to the sink, Lacey sipped her wine, and her mind went to the Knightsbridge Auction House job offer. She'd put it on the back burner during the investigation, just like she had her search for her father. But now that the case was solved, these life matters needed to be handled.

She stood, her mind in deep contemplation, and collected up the rest of the crockery. She carried it over to where Tom was loading the dishwasher.

"Here, let me do that," she told him. "You cooked."

"Yes, but you solved a murder. All I did was make a mushroom roulade and bake a zillion ghost-shaped gingerbread cookies."

She kissed him affectionately. "You've done quite enough for the day."

Tom smiled warmly. "In that case, do you mind if I retire early? I'm exhausted."

Lacey chuckled. "Of course not. I'll be up soon."

Tom pecked her cheek, then headed upstairs.

Lacey filled the dirty crockery into the dishwasher. She was on such a high from solving the case, she felt like she had enough energy to spring clean the house from top to bottom. She almost had enough energy to drive out to the countryside and knock on her father's door right that second, though she suspected his long-lost daughter showing up on his doorstep in the middle of the night might not go down so well from his perspective.

Just then, the sound of Lacey's phone ringing broke her from her thoughts.

"That'll be my mom," she said.

She was actually excited to speak to her mother about wedding plans. Now that the case was over, she was ready to throw herself into the planning. Besides, if she could get Superintendent Turner's approval, she could do anything.

But when she checked her phone screen, it wasn't Shirley's name flashing at her, nor an American area code. It was a Spanish one. And the name?

Xavier Santino.

At the sight of her former antiques contact, Lacey's stomach immediately began to churn. Why was he calling? Did he have news about her father?

It had been months since Xavier had kick-started her search for her father. Before he told her of the meeting the two had shared in New York City many years prior, Lacey hadn't even known whether her father was still alive. Xavier had helped her find clues and follow the crumbs right up until the point she cooled things off with him when she realized he was showing more interest in *her* than the mystery of her missing father.

If he was calling now, surely that meant he'd discovered something about her father.

As his name blinked at her on the screen, she deliberated over answering the call. She'd managed perfectly well without Xavier's help over the last couple of months—tracing Jonty Sawyer, and her father's property in Rye, and the subsequent address she'd sent her wedding invitation to—so it wasn't like she needed him anymore. But what if Xavier had found out something important about her father? Something earth-shattering? Something like his death?

From his basket, Chester barked, giving his customary reminder that she hadn't yet answered her phone.

Lacey's thumb hovered over the red button. She was about to reject the call when curiosity got the better of her. She just couldn't help herself. She pressed the green button.

The call connected with a crackle.

"Lacey?" came Xavier's soothing Spanish voice in her ear. "I have news."

CHAPTER TWENTY EIGHT

Lacey gripped her phone tightly in her hand, feeling tense all over. "I have news" wasn't exactly her favorite conversation starter. In her experience, such a statement usually ended in the announcement of a death or divorce.

"What news do you have?" she said into the receiver. "Is it about my father?"

"Actually, no," Xavier replied. "I am calling about my own family."

It took a moment for Lacey to recalibrate. She'd so been anticipating bad news that it took a moment to adjust, and for the anxiety to ebb from her body.

"Oh?" she asked, curiously. "What about them?"

"I thought you may be interested to know that the collection of maritime pieces I was trying to reunite has been completed," Xavier announced. "I found the last piece of my great-grandfather's antiques last week."

"Oh, Xavier!" Lacey exclaimed. "What fantastic news!"

Xavier had been trying to reunite his family's lost heirlooms for years.

"Thank you. There is a maritime museum in Verona interested in displaying it," he continued.

"That's wonderful," Lacey replied. "I'm just—I'm thrilled for you." Then she paused. "But why are you calling me about it?"

"I just… I wanted you to know," Xavier replied. "I wanted to hear your voice."

Lacey hesitated.

"Xavier, you know I'm engaged," she said.

"Yes—yes, of course." He faltered. "And congratulations. I suppose we have good news all around."

His tone had changed, Lacey noted. He sounded more stilted.

"Well, anyway," he continued, changing course, "I hope you can take my story and know it is possible to piece things together. I wanted my story to help you resume your search for your father."

"I did resume it," Lacey confessed. "And I think I'm really close to finding him. I have an address. I'm planning on going to see him, once I've attended to some business here."

"That's, well, that's great," Xavier said, though it was clear to Lacey her admission of having continued the search without him had hurt his feelings.

"A happy ending," he continued, sounding anything but. "Happy enough, at least. I suppose all that's left to say is *ciao*."

"I suppose so. Goodbye, Xavier."

The dial tone sounded before she'd even got out the last syllable.

Lacey twisted her lips and sighed. She felt bad for having shoved Xavier aside, but it was the right thing to do in order to be respectful to Tom. She was soon to be married. Tom had to be her priority.

She resumed stacking the dishwasher. But as she did, something Xavier had said during their call kept playing on her mind. He'd mentioned a museum in Verona, which had put her mind to the Macabre Museum Alaric owned in London.

He'd once owned it with Eldritch before the two fell out, according to Madeleine. Indeed, Eldritch had confirmed enough during her interrogation of him. The two had parted ways, that much was indisputable, but Eldritch's take on it was they had a friendly, rather than competitive, rivalry. It occurred to Lacey now that she hadn't actually researched it for herself. She'd just relied on word of mouth. When she'd done that before with Ash the mixologist, the information had turned out to be incorrect.

With a sudden niggling need to tie up all the loose ends, Lacey abandoned the dishwasher loading and opened her laptop.

She went online and typed *Macabre Museum* into the search bar. She quickly found Alaric's website. Its landing page was now taken over by a tribute to him—a large PR photo of him in his long black cape holding a candle, a nicely written obituary in floaty gothic handwriting, and a large public announcement message saying the museum would remain closed until further notice. In a column at the side of the page, Lacey noticed several links to other businesses under the heading of *FRIENDS*. The first on the list, right at the top, in prime position, was a link to a business called *Von Raven's*.

"Friends, huh?" Lacey wondered aloud, as she clicked the link that was quite obviously for Eldritch's business.

A new page filled her screen. The background was black, and decorated with oil drawings of ravens. *Can You Escape Von Raven's Lair?* the title read.

Lacey frowned as she began to scan the webpage. She quickly realized Von Raven's was not a museum at all. Eldritch's business was, in fact, some kind of a spooky-themed panic room, a sort of immersive haunted house experience. Quite different from the rival museum she'd been led to believe he'd split from Alaric to open.

"But in that case, they're not really in competition," Lacey mused aloud. "They run completely different ventures."

Madeleine must have misunderstood the nature of the two men's rivalry. Maybe the bad blood between them had nothing to do with their respective businesses being in competition, but simply because of how they'd parted ways in the first place.

But as her eyes scanned the matching column at the side of Eldritch's page, also entitled *FRIENDS,* where the first link, in prime position, was for the Macabre Museum, Lacey's frown grew even deeper. It was just like how she and Suzy supported one another, by displaying posters and flyers in their own businesses. This was the digital equivalent of that.

"It certainly doesn't look like there was bad blood between them," she murmured.

In fact, the information on the websites seemed to corroborate more with Eldritch's story than Madeleine's.

Had he and Alaric really had a friendly rivalry after all? And what about his claim he didn't steal the grimoire, because he didn't want to display it, and that he'd only been trying to inflate the price to mess with Alaric? An immersive panic room business didn't need expensive antique props. The grimoire would be of no real use to him at all.

Lacey sat back against the chair, her mind turning over as she tried to process the disjointed pieces of evidence. A horrible feeling began to churn inside of her. Was it possible she'd made a mistake accusing Eldritch? If he had no need for the grimoire, and no prior vendetta against Alaric, then the MO she'd attributed to him fell apart.

And yet everything pointed so neatly to him. He'd even admitted he'd gone to the island the night of Alaric's death, to "scare" him into believing the curse of the grimoire. But was it at all possible that Eldritch was telling the truth? That he'd only embellished his alibi because he knew how guilty he looked?

Suddenly her absolutely firm belief began to falter. And whenever Lacey realized there was a chance, even a slim one, that the case wasn't cracked, she felt compelled to see it to the end.

Which led to the all-important question. If Eldritch wasn't the killer, then who was?

Lacey began to search through her mind, trying to pinpoint where exactly in the investigation she'd become fixated on Eldritch.

"After the telephone call with Madeleine," she said. "She told me they were rivals. That was the moment I changed course." She looked again at the word *FRIENDS* on the website. "Madeleine must've misunderstood." Then she swallowed hard. "Or lied..."

An uneasy discomfort swept through Lacey and her stomach dropped. She didn't want to even entertain the thought, but had the sweet, polite young goth girl deliberately misled her? Had she diverted her attention from the real culprit by sending her on a wild goose chase?

Her hands began to shake as she went to her history tab and clicked on Madeleine's article on the grimoire. There at the bottom of the article, in neat, calligraphy-style writing, was her signature: *Madeleine Jourdemayne.*

"Wait..." Lacey said aloud, sitting up straight as a thought hit her. "Jourdemayne. Jourdemayne. That reminds me of something."

She grabbed her notebook and wrote it down. She stared at the word, then circled the first syllable.

"*Jour*," she said. "It's French. It means day, like *bonjour*, good day."

The cogs of her mind began whirring in overdrive. She was close to something, but she couldn't quite put it together.

"*Main* is hand," Lacey continued. "And *de*. *De* means of. Day of hand."

She went onto a surname tracking website and typed in *Jourdemayne*. She got a hit and pulled up the page.

Likely from Old French jour de main *meaning day of hand, or "day laborer."*

"Day laborer!" Lacey exclaimed, almost falling out of her chair. "That's where I heard it before. Day laborer! Just like the Ouvrière family who wrote the grimoire. The Ouvrières and the Jourdemaynes ... are the same family!"

157

She gasped for breath, suddenly going into overdrive. She continued reading, impatient with how slowly her eyes were moving, her heart racing rapidly.

Purported to have been brought to England from France by persecuted ouvrières (day workers) who were frequently scapegoated as witches. Later famously associated with Margery Jourdemayne, burned at the stake for witchcraft in Smithfield, 1441, and ancestor Violet Jourdemayne, hanged by public gallows for witchcraft, in Ippledean, 1684.

Lacey stood so quickly her chair tipped backward. The author of the grimoire, who wrote the book in Old French, was an Ouvrière, a poor laborer accused of witchcraft. Her ancestors had fled France for England because of the persecution, changing from Ouvrière to the Anglicized version Jourdemayne in the process, only to be persecuted here as well. Madeleine was a Jourdemayne, related to both Violet Jourdemayne *and* the author of the grimoire!

Madeleine *had* come to the auction for the grimoire all along…

Lacey ran through the facts in her mind. Madeleine had been checked into Carol's B&B, rather than the Lodge with the rest of the goth group. So Lacey hadn't corroborated her alibi, nor even considered the fact she wasn't on the surveillance footage at the Lodge. In fact, Lacey had been so won over by the young girl, she hadn't even suspected her in the first place.

But Madeleine had lied. She had tried to deflect Lacey's attention away from her at every step of the way, first by pretending to be at the auction by accident, then by acting shy and polite, and finally by pointing the finger of blame at other people. There was only one reason for that. To find a scapegoat. To turn the attention away from the real killer. Herself…

Suddenly, Lacey heard Finnbar's voice repeating in her mind. *"There's this whole legend about how the thirteenth daughter of the thirteenth daughter is a witch, and can invoke Violet's power by sacrificing a charlatan on La Toussaint."*

Lacey's heart flew into her throat. Adrenaline pounded through her. Madeleine Jourdemayne thought she was a witch, the thirteenth daughter. Alaric was her sacrifice! She was the killer!

Lacey had sent the wrong guy to jail. While all the police's resources were taken up by Eldritch, there'd be no one on the tail of the real killer. Madeleine was still out there, on the loose.

Then Lacey gasped as a sudden horrible thought struck her. Gina had said at dinner that the purple-haired goth girl was stopping by that night.

Her dear, cursed friend was in serious danger.

CHAPTER TWENTY NINE

Lacey didn't even stop to put on her rain mac. She wrenched open the back stable door and raced into the dark, cold evening, desperate with worry that her dear friend was in danger.

She must've woken Chester in her haste, because he suddenly appeared beside her legs, keeping pace with an expression of confusion as she pounded across the dewy grass to Gina's house. She'd done all of that work at the hotel, just to distract the cops, endanger her friend, and anger Suzy. She had been tricked, and so had the whole town. She had to make things right.

She reached Gina's back door and hammered her fist on it incessantly. "Gina! Gina, are you there?"

There was no answer. Lacey stepped back and peered up at the windows of Gina's cottage. The lights were on, beaming yellow glow across the lawn. She was definitely home. Then why wasn't she answering?

"Gina!" Lacey cried again, her panic mounting. She pounded her fists harder against the wooden door. "It's Lacey! Open up! Please!"

"Lacey?" came a voice from behind her.

Lacey's heart jumped into her mouth, and she swirled on the spot to come face to face with Gina, dressed in her pajamas and wellington boots, holding a watering can.

Relief flooded through Lacey. Of course. Gina was a strong proponent of "lunar gardening" and always watered her plants beneath the moonlight.

Lacey let out a tense sigh and grasped her friend, pulling her into an embrace. "Thank goodness you're okay."

"Of course I'm okay," the older woman said, sounding bemused as she patted Lacey's back. "Whatever is the matter with you?"

Lacey let her go. "Is Madeleine here?" she asked. Her breath was still labored from the panic and the sprint across the lawns.

"She already left," Gina said. Her eyebrows inched closer to her hairline as she stared at Lacey standing barely dressed on her back stoop. She set down the watering can and unlatched the back door.

"Come in out of the cold and tell me what's going on. Was there a problem with Madeleine's payment for the ram's skull or something? I know I made a mistake with the payment for the grimoire, but I'm absolutely certain I didn't fudge anything else."

Lacey didn't follow her inside the bright, warm kitchen, staying instead on the doorstep.

"Did she tell you where she was going?" she asked.

"Home," Gina replied, looking confused that Lacey was refusing to budge. "At least I presume so. I believe her exact words were, 'I'm heading back to where I belong.' To be honest, she was in a bit of a state. The poor girl was crying her eyes out. I didn't realize I'd had such an impact on her—"

"She thinks she's the thirteenth daughter," Lacey blurted. "From the legend Finnbar told us about. I did some more research after you left, and it all came together. I'm really sorry to tell you this, Gina, but I think Madeleine is the killer." She shook her head. "Not think. I know. I know she is the killer."

Gina's features turned from perplexed to horrified offense. "What on earth are you talking about? Madeleine isn't capable of such a thing! Eldritch is the killer. That's why he's sitting in a jail cell right now. The case is solved. Why are you trying to meddle in it again and accuse a sweet innocent girl?"

Lacey shook her head with exasperation. "Because I was wrong. It turns out that Violet Jourdemayne is a descendant of the author of the grimoire, the French Ouvriere family Finnbar told us about. Madeleine must've come here on some kind of pilgrimage to get her ancestors' grimoire back. She believes she's the thirteenth daughter of the thirteenth daughter! And since Alaric didn't actually believe in witchcraft, that made him the charlatan from the legend. The one who needed to be sacrificed."

Gina raised her eyebrows. "I think you've drunk a bit too much wine tonight, missy. Finnbar was telling us the plot of a bad seventies horror movie. Madeleine wouldn't sacrifice anyone!"

"Then why was she crying when she said goodbye earlier?" Lacey challenged.

"Because she's leaving," Gina replied, testily.

"Right. She's leaving for good. She's 'heading back to where she belongs,'" Lacey said, using air quotes to emphasize Madeleine's own words, and twisting her lips with consternation as she tried to work out

161

what precisely that meant. "She must think she can cross over to some other realm or something…"

Panic began rising in her chest again. But Gina clearly didn't want to believe it. She shook her head resolutely.

"I didn't think you even believed in witchcraft and curses and the spiritual," she said.

"I don't," Lacey told her. "But Madeleine clearly does." She struck on another thought. Finnbar said the sacrifice was supposed to take place on La Toussaint, the French equivalent of the day of the dead. Wasn't that tonight? Right now?

"Gina," she said, with a gasp. "It's La Toussaint, isn't it? That's the night in the legend. That's why Madeleine was crying. She's going to kill again, in order to perform the ritual to imbue herself with Violet Jourdemayne's powers! Are you sure you have no idea where she is?"

Gina's eyes dropped. "The ruins…" she said, quietly. "She said she wanted to look out over the ocean one last time." Her voice cracked. "Oh, Lacey. You don't think… you don't think she's going to hurt herself, do you?" Behind her spectacles, her eyes filled with tears.

"Not if I get to her first," Lacey replied. She stepped back off the step, filled with determination. "Call the station. Tell them I was wrong about Eldritch. I'm going to find Madeleine."

She turned, ready to bolt.

"Take this!" Gina cried from behind her. She shoved her famous bright yellow fisherman's jacket out the door.

Lacey grabbed it and slipped it over her shoulders. Then she hurried toward the cliff path, leaving her fretting friend behind her to contemplate all she'd just learned.

*

The cliff path was slippery from the rain. Lacey slid on the chalky pebbles as she hurried down toward the beach. Chester, on the other hand, descended with the grace of an ibex. He was clearly taking this new development very seriously, as he'd stuck close by Lacey ever since she'd bolted out her back door, leaving her fiancé snoring upstairs.

Chester reached the beach first, hopping down onto the sand and turning to bark at her, as if encouraging her to hurry up. Lacey jumped the final few feet to the beach and planted her feet in the sand. Without pausing, she began to run in the direction of the island.

162

It felt eerily desolate on the beach. There was no one else around, and the only light came from the almost full white moon above. Dotted around the beach were the remains of the bonfires the goth groups had congregated around on their first night in Wilfordshire. Lacey had thought back then that it looked as if they were performing rituals. Now, with all she'd just learned, she was quite confident they had been.

Across the still, black ocean emerged the silhouette of the medieval ruins. The sandbar that connected the mainland to the island was out, a sliver of pale sand in an otherwise black sea.

"We're in luck, Chester," she told her pooch.

She wasn't exactly a strong rower since Tom usually took the rowing duties upon himself, so she was relieved to know she wouldn't have to brave the ocean and could merely run across. But what might be waiting for her on the other side was the real worry…

She pulled Gina's rain jacket tight against the elements, and bolted across the long sand-bridge for the island. Chester bounded along at her heels, his fur becoming wet from ocean spray that clung in tendrils from his belly.

When Lacey reached the island, she ran straight for the ruins. She'd found them spooky enough before with Tom and Gina for company, but they were even scarier now she was alone. Wind howled through the crumbling stone corridors like the wailing song of ghosts.

Lacey tried to ignore her terror, reminding herself the real danger here was corporeal, and came in the form of a very confused young woman who thought she must perform dangerous, murderous, and potentially suicidal rituals to become a witch.

She raced through the twisting labyrinthine corridors and half crumbled rooms, searching the shadows for any sign of the young woman. Chester boldly sniffed the dark crevices, in case she was hiding, but neither human nor dog found a thing.

Am I too late? Lacey thought fearfully. *Has Madeleine already performed her spell?*

Just then, she spotted something glowing above her. She squinted through the gloom and realized, right at the top of the tower, there was a light. The smell of smoke lingered in the air.

"It's a bonfire…" Lacey murmured.

She couldn't help the awful imagery that popped into her head, of the Violet Jourdemayne effigy burning in the flames at the Lodge, and the real woman who'd met a truly grisly end. An uneasiness churned in her stomach.

She headed for the spiral steps and bounded up them, one hand against the cold stone walls to steady herself from the slippery stone.

When she reached the top, icy cold wind ripped through her hair and clothes, so powerful it threatened to push her right off the top of the tower. She gasped against it, feeling like she'd just been plunged headfirst into the ocean.

Exhausted and panting, Lacey swiped her hair from her eyes and surveyed the scene. At the far side of the tower, a small bonfire burned, though it appeared to be struggling to stay alight as it was battered by the gale force wind. Standing beside it, silhouetted by the light, was a slim, diminutive female figure. Madeleine.

"Madeleine!" Lacey cried over the wind. "Stop!"

The girl swirled on the spot with surprise. She was holding the grimoire open in her hands.

There was no doubt about it in Lacey's mind now. Madeleine was the thief of the grimoire and the killer of Alaric Moon.

"Lacey?" Madeleine cried with astonishment. "What are you doing here?"

"I figured it out," Lacey yelled in return. "I know what you did. I know why you did it. It's over. You need to stop."

Madeleine faltered. She stared at Lacey, her eyes as wide as the moon above her. She looked like a rabbit caught in the headlights, like a frightened, timid young girl who'd gotten in way over her head.

"I don't know what you're talking about," she replied, lying poorly.

The wind died down, and Lacey took a cautious step closer.

"Alaric," she said. "You stole the grimoire from him."

"No," Madeleine said firmly. "I took back what was mine. He had no right to stake a claim to it. The book was stolen from my ancestors, and profited from by the very people who persecuted them."

The passion and pain in her voice was evident. Lacey couldn't help but feel for this young woman and the bizarre, twisted logic that had led her to this place.

"I understand," she said, trying her best to defuse the situation. "If I'd known, I would've given the book to you. You didn't have to kill for it."

"I didn't kill for it!" she cried, desperately. "I liked Alaric. I didn't want him to die." She lowered her gaze to the grimoire in her hands. "But *they* did." Her voice lowered. "*She* did."

Lacey frowned with confusion. "Do you mean... Violet?"

"Yes," Madeleine said. "She was acting through me. She was the one who pushed Alaric off the tower. She was channeling me, using me as a proxy. She set this whole thing in motion. I had no choice but to follow the signs."

Lacey had heard some crazy things during this Halloween season, but this was by far the creepiest. Madeleine truly did believe she was the thirteenth daughter from the legend, and that she was being pushed along some kind of path by her magical ancestors.

"I had to follow the signs," she said again, sounding decidedly mad. "And it all came together perfectly, didn't it, Lacey? Not even a skeptic like you could deny that."

She was right. There were some very strange coincidences at play, Lacey had to admit. The grimoire had fallen into her possession by complete accident—had it not, it would have remained at the Ducking Stool in Ippledean unnoticed. Then she'd chosen to use the image of the grimoire on her website when she could've picked the skeleton or the taxidermy squirrel in his dinner jacket to advertise her auction. The image was picked up immediately by Madeleine's online circle of Violet Jourdemayne fanatics. And then there was Alaric, the charlatan who pretended to believe in witchcraft for business purposes, who'd ended up winning the coveted spell book. And the final piece of the puzzle? The ghost tour being unexpectedly cancelled, leaving Madeleine with a sudden open opportunity to strike.

"I didn't want to be a killer," came Madeleine meek voice, breaking through Lacey's thoughts. "One little push is all it took. My ancestors arranged everything for me. It all fell into place. I followed the charlatan here after he bought the grimoire. We were alone up here. I had no choice." Her voice cracked. Her eyes brimmed with tears.

Lacey couldn't help but feel compassion for her. She was confused. So, so confused.

The wind began to rise again.

"You have no idea how hard it is to be alone," Madeleine called against it. "To have no one believe you. To distance themselves from you just because you're a witch. I've had to live my whole life knowing my ancestors were brutally murdered just because of who they were. Because of something that I am, too. I've spent my whole life hiding. In the shadows. The only people I could even talk to were other Violet Jourdemayne fans online. I didn't plan any of it. You believe that, don't you? I had no choice. There are powers greater than myself at play."

"Madeleine," Lacey said, pleadingly. "You don't have to just go along with this. You can stop now."

She shook her head of purple hair. "I can't. It's too late. The wheels are in motion. I'm just a pawn. I have to finish the ritual and cross over to the other realm."

"Please," Lacey begged. "Whatever you're planning on doing, please don't do it."

Tears spilled from Madeleine's eyes, making the reflection of the bonfire in them dance and waver.

"You know what I'm going to do," she said, sounding suddenly resigned. Defeated. "You've already worked it out." She looked down at the grimoire in her hands. "Once I finish the incantation, there's just one thing left to do." She turned her face to the bonfire and stared dejectedly into the fire. "Step into the flames."

CHAPTER THIRTY

Lacey stared, aghast, as Madeleine turned her eyes down to the grimoire and began reading from it in a low murmuring voice. She had to do something. Not because she believed in any of it, but because Madeleine did, and she was moments away from leaping into the flames of her bonfire!

Lacey racked her brains for a plan, for anything that might prevent Madeleine from carrying out her gruesome act. She suddenly remembered something Finnbar had shown her during his research— the front page of the *Wilfordshire Weekly* paper. In it, they'd claimed the book was a fake, and had the quote from Jeff Peters the pawnbroker to back it up. Maybe, just maybe, if Lacey was able to plant a seed of doubt over the book's authenticity in Madeleine's mind, she'd be able to buy some time. Surely not even Madeleine would throw herself into the fire if she suspected the grimoire might be fake.

"Madeleine, stop!" Lacey cried. "The incantation you're reading isn't real. It's gobbledygook. The grimoire is a fake."

Madeleine faltered but only momentarily. She looked slightly rattled, but continued on, her voice stronger now.

"It's fake!" Lacey cried again, the wind trying to extinguish her words.

"You're lying!" Madeleine shouted, angry now by Lacey's interruption. "You're trying to stop me from crossing over to the next realm."

"There is no next realm," Lacey insisted. "And even if there was, that book isn't the way to get there. It isn't real. I can prove it, if you'll let me."

Madeleine's eyes twitched up from the grimoire. She stopped reading the incantation. "How?"

"It's in the local papers," Lacey said, rummaging in her pocket with her freezing cold hands that seemed unable to grip. She pulled out her cell and held it toward Madeleine. "Check for yourself. It's on the *Wilfordshire Weekly* website. Here!"

Madeleine looked skeptical, but she nodded. Lacey chucked her phone the small distance between them and Madeleine caught it.

Lacey watched as the girl's eyes darted from left to right, reading the scathing article in the *Wilfordshire Weekly* about Lacey being a phony. The longer she read, the more pained expression her expression became.

Suddenly, her eyes snapped up with anguish. Fury burned behind them. "You bought the book from a pawn shop? For twenty pounds? And sold it on for seventy thousand?"

Lacey nodded. "Yes. It's true. It's just some cheap knockoff from a pawn shop."

Madeleine's features fell. She looked desolate. "But then... that means... everything was wrong? The signs. The prophecy." She held the phone up high. "If this is true, then I killed Alaric for no reason!"

With her arm stretched up to the sky, the cell phone suddenly lit up and began to ring.

Madeleine paused. She lowered the phone. Then she looked up at Lacey and narrowed her eyes. "The Wilfordshire police are calling you."

Lacey suddenly remembered her instructions to Gina, to call the police and tell them where she was going.

Madeleine answered the call and put it on speakerphone.

"Lacey?" came Superintendent Turner's voice. "We're on the island. Tell us where you are. We're trying to pick up the GPS."

Madeleine's gaze snapped up to Lacey with fury. She threw the cell phone into the flames.

"You!" she bellowed suddenly, pointing a finger of accusation at Lacey. "Now I see it. You're the charlatan!"

The word hit Lacey like a blast of icy wind.

"All along, it was you!" Madeleine screeched. "My ancestors *are* guiding me, just not in the way I thought. I didn't need to kill Alaric or read from the grimoire. Because it's YOU who I'm supposed to sacrifice. On this night, La Toussaint, YOU, the one who mocks me and my ancestors, who profits from our tragedy, the real charlatan must die!"

Crap, Lacey thought. That had backfired spectacularly.

Madeleine pounced forward and grabbed Lacey by her forearms. Her fingers were like talons, latching painfully on to Lacey's arms and dragging her closer.

168

Chester began barking feverishly, the noise more high-pitched and frantic than Lacey had ever heard from him. She knew why. There was nothing he could do. The slippery stone tower was perilous. One false move, and both she and Madeleine would plunge from the tower top to the beach below, and end up like Alaric in a pile of twisted limbs.

"Stop!" Lacey cried, feeling Madeleine's fingertips boring into her. "I'm not the enemy."

Madeleine's dark eyes looked deranged. Something in her had snapped. The realization that Alaric had been killed for nothing? That the grimoire might have been a fake all along? Whatever it was, Madeleine looked like someone who'd lost all hope.

As they grappled atop the tower, Chester barked his little heart out. Lacey was so close to the edge, she got vertigo.

She pushed back against Madeleine and staggered, trying to gain a bit of distance from the perilous fifty-foot drop. But Madeleine was stronger than her. Despite her diminutive frame, she had nothing left to lose, and that was giving her all the strength she needed.

She spun Lacey around, her teeth clenched, and began to push her back. Lacey felt flames lick at her clothes. She was so close to the bonfire, to the flames. She was just seconds from being incinerated just like Madeleine's witchy ancestors had been.

Suddenly, the heavens opened and the rain began to fall in a downpour. From behind, Lacey heard the telltale hiss of the bonfire being extinguished.

"No!" Madeleine cried, her eyes darting over Lacey's shoulder to the bonfire behind, being quenched.

Moving at the speed of light, she shoved Lacey aside and leapt into the fire.

Lacey fell against the wet stones, hard, her palms slamming into the jagged rock. She felt her skin slice against the abrasive surface and screamed—not for herself, but for Madeleine.

Mustering all her strength, Lacey heaved herself to her feet and ran forward, grabbing hold of Madeleine's shoulder. She pulled, dragging her back and free of the flames, just as they were finally extinguished by the rain.

The two women tumbled back together, hitting the hard rock with a thud. They lay winded and entangled, in a strange sort of embrace. From above, the rain lashed them.

That's when Lacey heard Madeleine begin to weep. Her clothes were singed, steaming, and soaked, and her shoulder began to shake as sobs overcame her.

"It's okay," Lacey soothed. "You're all right now."

Then suddenly, a beam of a flashlight shone right in Lacey's eyes.

"Police!" cried Superintendent Turner. "Nobody move!"

CHAPTER THIRTY ONE

Lacey sat drenched and shivering in the waiting room of the Wilfordshire police station. Beth Lewis came out from the back area and handed her a Styrofoam cup of tea. It was milky looking, and clearly weak.

"Sorry. The vending machine's on the blink," the detective said.

Lacey didn't care. She was grateful for the warmth. She cupped it in both her hands.

"Is Madeleine okay?" she asked.

Beth took one of the hard plastic seats beside Lacey. "She's at the hospital. She's burned, but okay. It would've been much worse if you hadn't been there to save her."

Lacey shrugged. "Me. Or fate."

Beth frowned. "Fate?"

"The rain," Lacey said. "It would've been a whole lot worse otherwise."

She mulled it over. Maybe there was some truth to Madeleine's belief that her ancestors were leading her, only they were leading her away from harm. Perhaps they were trying to get her to live; while they had had their lives so cruelly taken from them, they wanted her to survive.

"How did you guys work out where I was?" Lacey asked. "Madeleine threw my cell in the fire to stop the GPS."

"It was Chester," Beth said. "We heard him barking."

Lacey looked over at the soggy, sleeping dog on the seat beside her. "He's a hero."

"Speaking of your cell," Beth said. She produced a large black molted lump in an evidence baggie and held it out to Lacey. "Might be time for an upgrade."

Lacey flashed her a weary smile and took the evidence baggie. "I think you might be right."

Just then, Lacey heard the internal door click open, and Eldritch Von Raven—aka Richard Bird—came strolling out. He'd spent a good few hours in jail because of her, so Lacey wasn't surprised when he gave her a cold look. He went to the reception desk and was handed back his possessions that had been confiscated.

He was about to walk away, ignoring Lacey, when he did a double take. He must've noticed her shivering and rain drenched, and was overcome with curiosity.

He walked over.

"What happened to you?" he said.

"Long story," Lacey said, her eyes on her milky tea.

"Why are you here?" he asked, clearly not satisfied with her evasive answer.

Lacey looked up and held his gaze. "I realized I'd made a mistake blaming you for killing Alaric and I felt a responsibility to put it right."

Eldritch's eyebrows twitched with confusion. He folded his arms. "Well. Yes. You did make a mistake," he said, sounding uppity. "What did you do?"

"I put it right," Lacey said, with a shrug. "I did what I was trying to do all along. I caught the killer. Madeleine."

Beth nudged her with her shoulder. "Got her to confess and everything," she said, with the air of a proud mother.

Lacey nodded and smiled shyly. After the night she'd had, she didn't much feel like accepting any praise.

"Madeleine?" Eldritch repeated, looking astonished. "Madeleine killed Alaric? But why?"

"For the grimoire," Lacey said. "She was convinced the book belonged to her ancestors, and that they were giving her signs or something."

"She's having a mental health evaluation at the hospital," Beth interjected. "She's exhibiting all the signs of an acute psychotic episode."

Eldritch frowned deeply, like he just didn't know how to process what he was hearing.

Just then, the cell phone he collected from the reception desk pinged. He glanced at it, then his eyes widened with surprise.

"Okay, nothing will surprise me now," he said as he scanned whatever was on the screen. "I got word back from the authenticator. The grimoire was a fake all along."

"It was?" Lacey asked, her eyes pinging open with surprise.

He nodded. "According to this email, it was just a prop from a movie."

Lacey gasped. So Finnbar had been right?

Just then, the automatic glass doors of the station swished apart. Gina came hurrying in, Boudica by her side.

Chester leapt up at the sight of her and Boudica and ran to his furry companion.

"Lacey!" Gina cried, running to her.

The two friends embraced.

"What happened?" Gina asked. "You're soaking!"

Lacey shook her head. "I'm fine. And Gina, this is important. The grimoire was fake all along. It was a movie prop from that seventies horror film Finnbar told us about. The curse you read was gibberish. You're in the clear."

"Thank goodness," Gina said, clearly relieved. "And Madeleine?"

Lacey nodded. "She'll be okay."

Gina nodded solemnly.

Just then, Lacey caught sight of the clock on the wall in the reception area. It was almost five a.m. A deep yawn took hold of her, and she could suddenly feel every ache and twinge in her body as the adrenaline gave way to exhaustion.

"Hold on, where's Tom?" Lacey suddenly asked her friend. "He didn't come with you?"

Gina's cheeks immediately went red. "I didn't knock!" she exclaimed. "My mind was in a tizz! Didn't you call him to say where you were?"

Lacey held up her phone. "My cell is a block of molten metal!" she exclaimed.

The two women gave each other wide-eyed looks.

"Quick, let's go!" Lacey cried.

What on earth would be going through her poor fiancé's mind when he awoke to discover her gone?

*

Dawn was rising as Gina drove up Lacey's driveway. Lacey was surprised to see every light on in the house.

Tom wrenched open the door and hurried down the path. He was wearing his night clothes.

"Where were you? I just woke up and you were gone!"

He grabbed her and held her tightly.

"Long story," Lacey said, folding into his arms. "I didn't realize I'd been at the station for so long. I'm sorry. I would've called you but my phone is just a molten hunk of plastic."

"Tell me what happened," Tom said, his eyes wide with astonishment.

He led her into the cottage. It was warm and bright, and smelled of his signature pastry, and faintly of Chester, and of comfort and home. The relief was overwhelming. She loved it here. Loved this place with every fiber of her being. She never wanted to leave. Not even, she suddenly realized, for a lucrative auctioneering job at one of the world's most revered auction houses…

"Do you want tea?" Tom asked, interrupting her thoughts as he guided her to the kitchen table like some kind of invalid.

She sank her weary, bruised body down into the dining chair.

"No, darling," she replied, feeling herself choke up with emotion. Her voice cracked.

Tom turned to her with a look of concern. "Oh, but Lacey, my love. You're crying!"

Lacey touched her fingers to her eyes. Indeed, her lashes were wet.

"I think they're happy tears," she told him.

"Happy tears?" he asked, sounding perplexed. "You just went through a terrible ordeal and you're crying tears of happiness?"

"Because I just realized," Lacey told him. "I never want to leave here. Not for all the money in the world. No job could ever tempt me away from what I have here. This perfect house. This perfect life. You."

Tom smiled, looking touched.

"Tom, I'm going to turn down the Knightsbridge job," she announced.

From the seat opposite, Tom hesitated.

"Maybe you should make that decision in the morning?" he said, finally. "Once you've had a nice warm bath and a cup of chamomile tea."

He stood and headed for the kitchen.

Lacey decided it was best to let him play the mother hen. She knew now in her heart what she wanted, but convincing Tom of that at this moment in time would be impossible. She decided to drop the conversation for now and pick it up again tomorrow morning.

Just then, Lacey spotted a piece of mail propped up against the centerpiece. It was handwritten and addressed to her.

"Tom, what's this?" she asked over her shoulder.

His teapot clattering ceased as he glanced over. "The letter? I'm not sure. It arrived yesterday but I forgot to tell you. I assume it's that job specification pack you were expecting from the auction house?"

Curiously, Lacey turned back to the envelope and picked it up. It didn't feel heavy enough to contain more than a single piece of paper.

For a brief second, she wondered if it was from her father. But no, the handwriting on the front was nothing like his.

She opened the envelope and retrieved the letter from inside, a neatly folded single sheet of paper.

Right away, the address in the top right told her the letter was not from the auction house in Knightsbridge at all, but from a museum in France. *La Musée de la Sorcellerie.*

Her intrigue spiking, she began to read.

Cease & desist.

To whom it may concern,

It has recently come to our attention that you claim to be in possession of a rare, ancient book, formerly belonging to a witch known in England as Violet Jourdemayne, and France as Violeta Ouvrier. We politely request you cease from continuing these claims. The real work is archived under lock and key here in a French museum. There is no evidence the Ouvrier family left France for England, nor that the witch you claim as your own was hanged in Ippledean. We take these slanderous claims very seriously, and will seek restitution if you continue to appropriate our culture and claim it as your own.

Lacey's mouth dropped open. She was stunned. So much for the grimoire being a fake; the museum was pretty much calling the entire Violet Jourdemayne story into question! And it sounded like they were blaming her for the whole of Wilfordshire believing the tale!

Tom came over with the teapot. The smell of freshly brewed chamomile floated out, giving Lacey an immediate dozy feeling.

"Well?" Tom asked. "Was it from the auction house?"

"Nope," Lacey said, yawning deeply. "It was just another twist in this long, twisty tale."

She reached across the table and took her fiancé's hand lovingly. Her life was perfect. She should never have allowed herself to be tempted by the job offer. This was where she belonged.

"Tom?" she said, giving his fingers a little squeeze.

"Yes, my love?" he replied.

"What do you think about a Celtic harp for the wedding?"

EPILOGUE

"Are you *sure* you're sure about this?" Tom asked.

Lacey held the big envelope in her hand. The job pack from the Knightsbridge auction house had arrived on her doorstep first thing that morning, but Lacey hadn't even opened it.

"I'm absolutely positively certain," she said with a nod.

Then she dumped it in the trash can.

The pack landed with a loud thud, reverberating through the metal.

Tom took her in his arms. "I guess that's that, then," he said. "The case is solved. Our future is decided. And there's going to be a Celtic harpist at our wedding."

Lacey leaned into him and grinned. "There's just one thing missing."

"Oh?" she heard him say.

"My father," she replied. She peered up at his side profile. "Tom, I want to go and meet him."

She'd been holding it back all this time, her plan to travel to the return address on the blank envelope her father had mailed her. Tom had been so skeptical that the envelope was a clue, she hadn't wanted to bring it up to him again. He must've assumed she'd just dropped the whole thing, that she'd continue putting it off indefinitely. But she had not. The whole while she'd been dealing with Eldritch and Madeleine and Alaric Moon, it had been burning in the back of her mind. If her experience on top of the medieval ruins had taught her anything, it was that she was far stronger than she realized. If she could wrestle a half-mad young woman out of the flames of a bonfire, she could certainly visit her long-lost father.

Tom's eyebrows rose halfway up his forehead. "You're going there? Now?"

"To the address on the envelope," Lacey said, with a decisive nod. "Now."

"But—but—" Tom stammered.

"I've been putting it off for too long," Lacey interjected. "It's time to rip off the Band-Aid. I need to know. I need to know if he will be walking me down the aisle in two months' time. And if not…" She shrugged. "Then I'll ask Frankie to do it."

Tom twisted his lips with anguish. "Lacey, I'm worried about you. You had quite a scare yesterday. Your bruises haven't even all come up yet. Are you sure this is a good idea?"

"I'm positive," Lacey said. "Even if he rejects me again, at least then I'll know. I'm going to go to the address. I need to do this."

"Okay," Tom said, with a relenting sigh. "Just know I'm here for you, no matter what happens."

Lacey took his hand and squeezed it. "I know you are."

She pushed up from the breakfast table and whistled for Chester. He came bounding over to her, his tail wagging excitedly. Together, they headed out of the cottage and got into the car.

They drove for what felt like forever, through the lush green hillsides of England. There was no turning back now, as far as Lacey was concerned. She needed to do this. Madeleine had made her realize just how preoccupied she was with her own past, and how blind one could become by believing the wrong thing. The truth was, she had no idea why her dad had left, or why he'd broken off contact with her. It didn't matter how many scenarios she came up with, there was only one way to ever know the truth. To ask him outright.

She turned down a small country road, barely wide enough for two cars to pass, the type with no markings and where the hedges encroach on each side trying to strangle you. It was as desolate as Lacey suspected from the type of man she presumed her father had become.

It was almost impossible to navigate. Her cell phone showed her in the middle of a field, though she was, of course, not. Clearly modern GPS had nothing to triangulate her against. She didn't even have a signal.

This place was completely cut off from everyone and everything.

She drew up beside a locked cow gate.

"This can't be the place," she said to Chester. "There's no way past."

She spotted the stile beside the gate. There was a way—just not for a vehicle. She would have to continue the rest of the journey on foot.

She parked, tucking her car against the side of the road, and stepped out into the brisk countryside air.

The rain from last night had turned the vegetation to a lush green color, and there was something beautiful in the bleak, desolate landscape. It was just the sort of place Lacey's favorite literary heroines would embark on tempestuous love affairs.

Chester slinked out of the car behind her, sniffing the air eagerly. Lacey was glad for his company. He was her most trusted companion.

With Chester sticking close beside her, Lacey climbed the stile and trudged along the footpath, which was little more than a bridleway trampled into the field by horses' hooves. The grass on either side was long and dewy. It felt like a wild, forgotten place.

Finally up ahead, Lacey spotted a small stone cottage, set in an estate made up of corrugated iron farm buildings and wooden sheds—presumably shelter for the cows. Somewhere deep inside of her, Lacey knew this was the place. After all her years of yearning, agonizing, searching... she was finally right where she needed to be, right where her father was. It was a day she'd never thought would come, and she felt herself becoming disembodied, like she'd slipped into some kind of dream.

She made her way across the muddy ground, squelching, slipping, and sliding as she went. Her father had clearly gone to a lot of effort to be cut off from the world. Lacey felt like she was completing an obstacle course.

Finally, she staggered up to the door of the cottage.

With her heart pounding in her chest, she raised her fist to the wooden door and knocked.

For a long while, all was silent. The only noise Lacey could hear was the blood pulsing in her ears. Her heart was racing so much, even her hands seemed to be beating in time.

Then she heard noise from the other side. A scritching sound. The scraping of a dead bolt being drawn across. The click of a latch. Then a low, deep creak, like the sound of rusted metal, as the door was slowly pulled open from the inside.

In the gap in the door, the face of a man appeared. The face belonged to a stranger, Lacey noted, but a stranger she knew intimately at the same time.

There was no mistaking it. It was him. Her father.

"Hi, Dad," she said.

A smile spread across his face. "There you are."

NOW AVAILABLE!

FRAMED BY A FORGERY
(A Lacey Doyle Cozy Mystery—Book 8)

"Very entertaining. I highly recommend this book to the permanent library of any reader that appreciates a very well written mystery, with some twists and an intelligent plot. You will not be disappointed. Excellent way to spend a cold weekend!"
--Books and Movie Reviews, Roberto Mattos (regarding *Murder in the Manor*)

FRAMED BY A FORGERY (A LACEY DOYLE COZY MYSTERY—BOOK 8) is book eight in a charming new cozy mystery series which begins with MURDER IN THE MANOR (Book #1), a #1 Bestseller with over 100 five-star reviews—and a free download!

Lacey Doyle, 39 years old and freshly divorced, has made a drastic change: she has walked away from the fast life of New York City and settled down in the quaint English seaside town of Wilfordshire.

November has arrived, bringing the crisp weather, farms, and the promise of Fall holidays, and Lacey is thrilled to be auctioning off a rare and priceless letter. But after selling it to an eager buyer, the letter turns out to be too good to be true—it's been forged, and the buyer wants his money back.

But the person who sold it to her is now dead.

Can the forgery and murder be connected?

Lacey, with her beloved dog, must solve the crime and unearth the source of the forgery before she herself is implicated and her business is taken away from her.

Book #9—CATASTROPHE IN A CLOISTER—is also available!

Fiona Grace

Fiona Grace is author of the LACEY DOYLE COZY MYSTERY series, comprising nine books (and counting); of the TUSCAN VINEYARD COZY MYSTERY series, comprising six books (and counting); of the DUBIOUS WITCH COZY MYSTERY series, comprising three books (and counting); of the BEACHFRONT BAKERY COZY MYSTERY series, comprising six books (and counting); and of the CATS AND DOGS COZY MYSTERY series, comprising three books (and counting).

Fiona would love to hear from you, so please visit www.fionagraceauthor.com to receive free ebooks, hear the latest news, and stay in touch.

BOOKS BY FIONA GRACE

LACEY DOYLE COZY MYSTERY
MURDER IN THE MANOR (Book#1)
DEATH AND A DOG (Book #2)
CRIME IN THE CAFE (Book #3)
VEXED ON A VISIT (Book #4)
KILLED WITH A KISS (Book #5)
PERISHED BY A PAINTING (Book #6)
SILENCED BY A SPELL (Book #7)
FRAMED BY A FORGERY (Book #8)
CATASTROPHE IN A CLOISTER (Book #9)

TUSCAN VINEYARD COZY MYSTERY
AGED FOR MURDER (Book #1)
AGED FOR DEATH (Book #2)
AGED FOR MAYHEM (Book #3)
AGED FOR SEDUCTION (Book #4)
AGED FOR VENGEANCE (Book #5)
AGED FOR ACRIMONY (Book #6)

DUBIOUS WITCH COZY MYSTERY
SKEPTIC IN SALEM: AN EPISODE OF MURDER (Book #1)
SKEPTIC IN SALEM: AN EPISODE OF CRIME (Book #2)
SKEPTIC IN SALEM: AN EPISODE OF DEATH (Book #3)

BEACHFRONT BAKERY COZY MYSTERY
BEACHFRONT BAKERY: A KILLER CUPCAKE (Book #1)
BEACHFRONT BAKERY: A MURDEROUS MACARON (Book #2)
BEACHFRONT BAKERY: A PERILOUS CAKE POP (Book #3)
BEACHFRONT BAKERY: A DEADLY DANISH (Book #4)
BEACHFRONT BAKERY: A TREACHEROUS TART (Book #5)
BEACHFRONT BAKERY: A CALAMITOUS COOKIE (Book #6)

CATS AND DOGS COZY MYSTERY
A VILLA IN SICILY: OLIVE OIL AND MURDER (Book #1)
A VILLA IN SICILY: FIGS AND A CADAVER (Book #2)
A VILLA IN SICILY: VINO AND DEATH (Book #3)

Made in United States
Orlando, FL
22 September 2024